The Railroad Murder Case

The Railroad Murder Case

R. M. LAURENSON

COACHWHIP PUBLICATIONS
Greenville, Ohio

The Railroad Murder Case, by R. M. Laurenson
© 2023 Coachwhip Publications edition
Cover: Jack Delano / Farm Securities Administration,
    Office of War Information photograph collection
    (Library of Congress)

First published 1948
Robert M. Laurenson, 1906-1982
CoachwhipBooks.com

ISBN 1-61646-570-0
ISBN-13 978-1-61646-570-4

1

Every railroad man knows that trouble comes in threes. Engineer Baxter, swaying with the buck and pitch of his big Malley, couldn't help but wonder about number three. One and two had been lucky. The Calumet brakeman who'd stepped in front of a yard engine could easily have been killed. And the cut of cars that had split a switch and fouled the main ahead of Number 42! Wow! If the Flyer hadn't pinched down for a hotbox, there'd have been a "corn field meet" for the books. But number three—?

He peered through a gust of rain, the last of a storm that had lashed him for miles, at a tiny speck of green. He reached for the whistle cord and shrieked a greeting to the tower operator, dimly visible at his lonely post. The drivers battered the rails of a crossing. The train leaned into a long curve, and disappeared into the night.

A mangy dog, busy with matters of importance to a mangy dog, trotted up the bank and picked his way over the tracks. He hesitated at the crossing and sniffed curiously at a crimson trickle that drip-dripped over the edge of a tie. Shaking the water from his coat with a convulsive shudder, he too disappeared into the night.

A star peeked through a hole in the clouds. The rumble of thunder grew faint in the distance. Peace settled over Zola Crossing.

A slender girl stood on the end of a pier that jutted into the lake and waved a handkerchief over her head. A little black dog squatted behind her and watched.

A speedboat snarled in from the center of the lake, white foam spewing from its bow. A short distance away it banked in a sharp, skidding turn. Drops of spray dotted the water almost to her feet, and the boat headed away from shore. Another skidding turn completed a figure eight and once more the boat headed inshore. Suddenly the roar of the exhaust died to a murmur. The boat seemed to stumble as the bow settled into the water. Slowly it drifted toward the pier.

A sandy-haired young man brought the mahogany beauty up to its berth with scarcely a jar. He cut the ignition switch, lit a cigarette and turned laughing blue eyes up to the girl.

"David Arnold," she said severely, "you'll be late for the train. It's four now and we must be on our way by six."

Arnold grinned at her. "Sorry, Mrs. Arnold. I had to try out Betsey." He patted the wheel of the speed boat. "She's a bird today. Carburetor jet did the trick. I wish the club regatta was next week instead of last."

"Please hurry, Dave. Daddy will be furious if we're late and delay one of his trains—even a minute. Come along, Cleo," she called to the dog.

Arnold nodded. "Be with you in a jiffy. Soon's I tie up Betsey."

He quickly moored the boat fore and aft and slipped a canvas hood over the cockpit.

While her husband completed his nautical chores, Joan walked rapidly toward the large stone cottage set several hundred feet from shore. She was oblivious to the beautiful setting: the white sandy shore line; the smooth lawn that sloped up to a flagstone terrace in front of the house.

Hurrying up the walk, she glanced at her watch. She was met at the door by a prim little woman, with a starched cap perched on her gray hair and a white apron tied at her waist over a severe black dress.

"Miss Joan," she said.

"Yes, Dooly, what is it?"

"D'you know yet when you'll be back?"

Joan thought a moment. "I really don't, Dooly."

"I'll hafta know, ma'am, on account of we're outa food."

"I know. We'll be in Chicago several days. Depends on Daddy, and how long it takes Dave to finish his business. I want to stop in Calumet for a day or so. I'll telephone you from Calumet. Will that do?"

"Yes ma'am. Guess so."

"We may have guests. The Snyders are coming back with us if Al can get away. I'll let you know about that too."

"Yes ma'am."

"Is Daddy packed yet?"

"No ma'am. He's takin' himself a nice long bath."

"Oh, dear! These men! I wonder if Mr. Johnson's ready?"

Mrs. Donovan's lips compressed into a thin line. She shrugged her shoulders.

"Wouldn't know, ma'am."

Joan glanced at her disapprovingly. "Now, Dooly, you shouldn't let your feelings show so plainly."

"Humph!"

"I'll see if I can hurry Dad. Close my bags, please, and then help Dave if you can. He'll need a tie or something."

Joan hurried across the pleasant room facing the lake. She smiled at an attractive woman of forty or so, who sat by a window reading.

"At least, Miss Arthur, you're ready. The perfect secretary."

A faint smile twisted her lips.

"I know your father, Miss Joan. I thought it best to be ahead of time and keep out of the way."

Joan tripped up the stairs. Strains of "Home on the Range" sung in a clear but off-key baritone rolled through the bathroom door. She waited for the singer to pause for breath, then rapped.

"Yes, what is it?"

"Daddy, it's getting late. Aren't you nearly ready?"

"Stop fussing! Can't I enjoy a bath in peace?"

"But you haven't packed yet, and we must leave soon."

"Pack! Haw! Take two minutes."

"Well, hurry."

Three quarters of an hour slipped by, filled with much scurrying about and closing of bags, before the luggage was stacked by the door, and the travelers were assembled. Mr. Richards was the last to appear. He stamped down the stairs and stopped in the door to the room where the others waited. He seemed to fill the doorway, his shoulders just clearing the jambs. A powerful hand brushed a speck of dust from his trouser leg. His jovial, ruddy face was twisted into a good-natured grin.

"All set? Let's go. Where's Johnson?"

Joan shook her head. "Haven't seen any sign of life next door since noon. I hope he's ready."

Richards grunted. "We'll go without him, then." He pulled a watch from his pocket and glanced at it briefly. "We've just time to make the train."

Joan straightened her father's tie. "And whose fault, Mr. Railroad President? I told you!"

Richards kissed her on the forehead. "Yes, my dear."

Arnold picked up a bag in each hand and started for the door. "How about Dorene? Isn't she going?"

Miss Arthur stiffened. Her lips showed thin and red in her white face. Joan frowned.

"No, she decided to stay here," she said.

"Just as well," grunted Richards, darting a quick glance at Arnold.

Mrs. Donovan fluttered about, brushing Miss Arthur's coat, finding Joan's handbag and supplying her with a handkerchief. Richards gathered up an armful of bags and they trooped out to a station wagon parked in the driveway.

A tall man leaned against a fender. He held a cigarette between tapered fingers. Blond hair, gray at the temples, was combed straight back, and a clipped mustache marked the line of his lips. He looked like the president of the Calumet National Bank, which he was. He nodded as the party gathered around the car.

"Well, Johnson," said Richards curtly, "see you made it. Dave, stow this junk in the back and let's be on our way."

Arnold complied, with the half-hearted assistance of Johnson. Richards fitted his bulk behind the wheel and Miss Arthur took the seat beside him with an air of assuming her proper position. Joan cuddled Cleopatra in her lap. Richards spun the car around the curved driveway, kicking up a spray of gravel.

The half-hour drive was made in almost complete silence. Autumn sunlight slanted through the trees fining the peaceful country road. Dry leaves swirled and eddied around the speeding car. A squawking chicken, deciding the other side of the road was the place to be, ducked between the wheels.

The station wagon approached a lonely, one-room building set beside a railroad track. A solitary Pullman stood on a siding a little distance from the building, smoke curling invitingly from a pipe at one end. Richards drove up beside the car and stopped.

The sun disappeared suddenly behind a bank of angry clouds as the travelers collected on the platform and sorted out their luggage. Richards turned to Arnold.

"Park the car in the shed, Dave. Check with the operator on 61. He'd better be on time!"

A white-coated porter scrambled down the car steps, his ebony face wreathed in a broad grin.

"Evenin' folks," he said. "Mistah Richards, suh, Ah wuz scairt yo' wuz gonna be late."

Richards let out a bellow. "Cliff, you rascal! You know me better'n that. What you got on that stove? It'd better be good, or I'll fire you!"

Cliff bobbed his head vigorously. "Yas suh. Chicken, suh. Roast chicken."

"Haw! Chicken!" Richards clapped Cliff on the back. "On second thought I'll raise your pay. Rassel this stuff on board, and then you mind that chicken. Come on, folks; Cliff's roast chicken is nothing to fool around with."

He helped Joan and Miss Arthur up the steps. "Let's see now," he said when they had all gathered in the lounge at one end of the car. "Joan, you and Dave take the stateroom. Miss Arthur, Johnson and I'll take a roomette each, and that'll leave one for Linden, when he gets here."

Arnold stepped into the lounge from the aisle. "Don't you want the stateroom, J. C.?" he asked. "That's your bunk."

Richards shook his head. "Not tonight. Full load. This'll work better,"

Nodding, Arnold picked up his bag and Joan's and set them in the stateroom. Joan followed him. She shook off her coat and hung it in a miniature closet. Seating herself before a tiny dressing table, she started to repair the damage of the auto ride. Arnold leaned over, slipped his arms around her and kissed her on the neck. Cleopatra rested her front paws on the edge of the bench and watched the caress.

"Glad you decided to go, Joanie," he said. "We'll step out and see the big city."

Joan smiled in the mirror, reached up and rumpled his hair with her fingertips. "That'll be fun, Dave. We haven't been to Chicago for quite a while. Hurry now. Mustn't spoil Dad's roast chicken!" She patted his cheek gently, and continued her beauty treatment.

Arnold, whistling softly, shucked his coat onto a berth and began the masculine equivalent of primping with lather brush and razor.

Joan gave her hair a final, minute adjustment, and stepped into the aisle just as a faint whistle blast broke the rural peace. A headlight poked a finger through the dusk.

Richards' door banged open and he dashed through the lounge to the observation platform. A big engine, clanking rhythmically, slid by on the main track. Richards leaned over the rail and waved to the grinning crew in the cab.

"Baxter, you son-of-a-gun!" he yelled. He pointed with mock severity to his watch. "Where you been?"

Baxter clasped his hands over his head and shook them in greeting.

"Hi ya, Dick!" he shouted. "Come on up and see if you can do better!"

"By heaven, I'll take you up on that," replied Richards, dropping to the ground and walking rapidly after the slow-moving train. It stopped at a switch a short distance beyond the private car. A brakeman hopped off the rear platform, flipped the switch lever, and waved his arm in a big circle. Slowly the train backed onto the siding, eased up to the car, and bumped it gently. Richards scrambled up the steps of the engine and disappeared into the cab.

In the car, Miss Arthur walked slowly into the lounge and settled into a corner of the davenport beside Joan. She glanced diffidently at Johnson seated across from her. A pair of pince-nez glasses were clipped to the bridge of his nose. The tense fingers of one hand gripped the pages of a financial magazine, while the other hand rhythmically massaged the arm of his chair.

Miss Arthur's forehead wrinkled, and her lips pursed in a disapproving pout. She tapped a cigarette, inserted it carefully into a short holder, and flipped a lighter on the table beside her. She shot a sidewise glance at Joan.

"Where's Mr. Richards?" she asked. "I thought he was here."

Joan chuckled. "He's gone up to the engine to play! Can't keep his hands off a throttle. And Baxter's an old pal of his."

"Your father's just a big boy," murmured Miss Arthur. "He'll never grow old."

Joan studied her for several minutes in silence. "You're very fond of Dad, aren't you, Miss Arthur?" she asked.

"Fond?" A slow flush rose from Miss Arthur's throat. She tapped the ashes from her cigarette. "I have great respect for him. Great respect." She glanced again at Johnson, almost venomously. "That's more than some people have!"

Johnson's hand missed a beat, then resumed its travel back and forth on the chair arm. He laid down his magazine and methodically began to polish his glasses.

"Daddy has great confidence in you," continued Joan. "He says you're a wonderful help to him."

"Confidence! Help!" snapped Miss Arthur. She caught her breath sharply. "Yes, I enjoy my work with him."

The train jerked violently, and then rolled forward.

"Goodness!" gasped Joan. "Dad's slipping. If Baxter started like that, Dad would bawl him out right!"

She was interrupted by a slight man of medium height who stepped into the lounge. His reddish brown hair was parted precisely in the middle, and he wore a severe black topcoat. He set his bag down and turned inquiringly to Joan.

"Good evening, Miss Joan," he said. "Miss Arthur—Johnson. Where's your father?"

Joan laughed softly. "Up front, playing train. He'll be back. Cliff!"

"Yassum?" replied Cliff, trotting into the lounge.

"Take Mr. Linden's bag, Cliff. He's to have the last roomette."

"Yassum." He hesitated a moment. "Dinnah's 'bout ready, Mis' Joan. An' Mistah Richahds ain't heah. What'll Ah do?"

"Go ahead and serve, Cliff. We're hungry."

Cliff shook his head dubiously. "Ah don' know, ma'am," he protested. "Mistah Richahds, he kinda p'ticular 'bout—"

"Don't worry about Dad. I'll handle him. You serve dinner."

"Yassum."

He disappeared after Linden, to reappear shortly with two folding tables. These he set up in the center of the car and, with a dexterous twist, spread a snowy cloth over them. Quickly, skillfully, he set the table for six. He was placing the last napkin when Richards appeared.

Richards' coat sleeves were pushed back, showing dirt-smudged shirt cuffs. His face was smeared with coal soot, and a happy grin.

Joan shook a finger at him. "Dad," she said, "you should be ashamed. You'd fire Baxter if he started the way you did."

Richards hung his head in shame. "Lousy, eh? . . . Chicken! Cliff, get that bird in here. I'm hungry."

"Yas suh. Comin' up, suh," replied Cliff, scurrying in with a load of plates. Richards disappeared into his room, and soon the sounds of splashing water filled the car. He returned a few minutes later, clean of hand, face and shirt. His eyes lighted on Linden and the grin faded. Linden's close-set eyes turned to the floor under the stare.

"Well, Linden," grunted Richards, "how'd you make out in St. Paul?"

Linden glanced quickly at Richards, and then away. He shook his head.

"Credit shot, eh? I'm not surprised. You know what that means?"

Linden nodded dumbly, while Miss Arthur and Johnson watched the encounter in surprise. Joan laid a restraining hand on her father's arm.

"Daddy, please!" she said.

"Okay," he growled. He turned to Johnson. "Where's your beautiful wife? She getting coy—for a change?"

Johnson again polished his glasses before answering. "No, I wouldn't say that. She wanted a few days of rest. She's had a busy week."

"Haw! Rest? She doesn't know what it is."

Cliff entered with a luscious brown chicken on a silver platter. Richards smacked his lips and waved to the others.

"Gather 'round, folks. Let's eat." He picked up the silver carving knife and set to work on the bird.

Dinner dragged on, with very little conversation. Linden toyed with his food, scarcely touching it. Johnson ate slowly, savoring each mouthful. But Richards pitched in like a farmhand. He ended up with the whole carcass on his plate. By the time the last morsel of meat had been searched for and consumed, his good humor had returned.

Dinner over, he slouched in a big chair and lit a cigar. "Mighty good, Cliff. Mix me my drink, and fix the others something. Leave a table. We'll shoot a little bridge. How about it, Joan?"

Joan shook her head. "Not tonight, Dad. I'm going to bed soon. I may read for a while."

Richards turned inquiringly to Miss Arthur. She too shook her head.

"I don't feel up to it, Mr. Richards."

"Okay, Dave, you and I'll give these two financial wizards a bridge lesson."

"All right, J. C.," replied Arnold, "only if you open with a two bid, I'll expect at least four and a half honor tricks!"

"Listen, you young pup," roared Richards, "don't tell me how to bid! Sit down and play. What'll it be, a cent a point?" He glanced at the other men. Johnson shrugged. Linden pawed at his chin, and nodded.

The men seated themselves around the table, while Cliff whisked a dust cloth over it, and produced cards and a score sheet. At a signal from Richards he filled the glasses and set a cigarette holder on an end-table. Miss Arthur watched the start of the game silently, and Joan thumbed through a newspaper.

The rubber dragged on. Richards ran the bidding to six no trump. Johnson coldly doubled. While Richards was playing the hand, Arnold lit a cigarette and went to the sideboard where he refilled his glass. He returned to the table as Richards laid down a spot in spades, finessed Johnson's king against ace-queen in the dummy, and claimed the rest of the tricks, making seven.

"Nice work, J. C.," said Arnold. "That'll help the score."

Richards chuckled. "Twenty-four dollars and ten cents. I'll take that—from Linden!"

Linden's face flushed. "You had all the luck," he snapped.

Joan rose, covering a yawn with her fingertips.

"I'm going to bed," she said. "Don't play too long, Dave."

He smiled at her and shook his head. "I won't."

Miss Arthur rose, excused herself, and followed Joan.

The bridge players settled down to the game. Linden played bitterly, making every bid and playing every card as though his life depended upon it. Johnson, aloof, detached, almost disinterested, gave him superb support. Richards played with the reckless abandon of a gambler ahead of the game.

In the middle of a tight four heart contract played by Arnold, Cliff stepped silently into the lounge and handed Richards a bit of paper folded into a square. Richards unfolded the paper and read the note through several times. He crumpled the sheet into a wad, dropped it into the big ash tray, and walked to the sideboard where he mixed another drink. He made no comment when Arnold missed a squeeze play and was set one trick. He made no comment a moment later when, neglecting to overcall, he allowed Linden to get an easy one no trump contract with part score.

While Linden, a triumphant smirk on his pasty face, played the hand, Johnson strolled to the rear door of the car and stepped out on the platform. Cleopatra, sniffing excitedly, danced to her feet and followed him.

Richards pitched his hand onto the table in disgust. "Okay, Linden," he said. "Your rubber. Hope you're happy." He quickly added the score. "You owe me ten dollars. Let's quit. Tomorrow's a big day." He extended one hand toward Linden, rubbing thumb against finger suggestively. "Ten dollars, please. Give."

Silently Linden handed Richards a bill.

Richards grinned at Arnold. "Nice work, Dave. You'll make a fair bridge player some day. Good night. See you tomorrow." He tucked the bill in his pocket, waved cheerfully, and disappeared through the door. Without a word, Linden followed him.

Johnson wandered in from the platform. He glanced at the deserted bridge table in surprise. "Well, game's over, eh?"

Arnold, sprawled in one end of the davenport, looked up from a magazine and nodded. "Yup. J. C. had enough."

Johnson clipped his glasses to his nose, selected a magazine from a pile on the book stand and seated himself comfortably in a big chair against the forward partition.

2

A telegraph sounder clattered away, unheeded, on a corner of the desk. A maze of tiny red and green lights twinkled in a panel mounted on one wall. John O'Conner, train dispatcher at ZA tower, studied the train sheet spread out before him.

A loudspeaker in the corner broke the silence.

"O. S. Paront!"

"O. K. Paront."

"Extra 24—arrived 9:13—departed 9:17. No work."

"O. K—Cicero?"

"Cicero."

"How's Number 6, George? Showed yet?"

"Comin' now, John. Let him go?"

"Yeah. He'll meet 13 at Marquette." O'Conner pushed a button on his telephone ringer.

"Hackett!"

"When's 10 called for, Steve?"

"Nine forty-five. Damn near make that figger too."

"He'd better."

O'Conner stretched lazily and touched a match to his pipe. A gong sounded and a red light flashed at one end of the track model. A telephone bell buzzed insistently. O'Conner flipped a switch on the table.

"ZA!"

"Hello ZA.—BN tower. Passenger Number 61—engine 3140—engineer Baxter—conductor Holland—eastbound with ten cars. OS at BN, 9:23. Treat him nice, Johnny. He's got Mr. Richards on behind."

"O. K., BN. Dicky's comin' home, eh?"

"Nope. Car's billed through to Chi. Tough way to travel, ain't it?"

"Tough. Thanks, Joe. I'll give him the railroad."

The speaker lapsed into silence, and for ten minutes O'Conner smoked peacefully. Suddenly the gong sounded and a red light appeared on the board. O'Conner looked up in surprise, reached for the telephone and dialed a number. In a few seconds a sleepy voice came over the wire.

"Hello."

"Morrison—O'Conner. Trouble at Perkins again. She just showed red. Take a look at it, will ya?"

"The heck with Perkins! And the heck with this railroad! I'm sick o' night calls."

"Take it easy, Morrie. Mosely said he'd clean ballast there tomorrow. Stay out there at Perkins, will ya? Stay till 61 gets by. He's draggin' Mr. Richards and if we delay him, there'll be the devil to pay."

"O. K.—O. K.," grumbled Morrison. "Whatta life!"

3

Marc Jordan, chief attorney for the C. M. Railroad, slouched behind the wheel of his weather-beaten Ford and guided it skillfully along the winding road. One lean hand lay negligently on the wheel and he fumbled through his pockets with the other.

"For heaven's sake, Marc, 'tend to business!" exclaimed the black-haired girl beside him. "Some day you'll kill yourself, and I don't want to be along. Here—take this." She handed him a freshly lighted cigarette.

"Thanks, Nora. This isn't fast. We'll have to be careful tonight. It's slippery."

"You know, darling, Webster wrote a book—a dictionary. Why don't you look up 'careful'? You'd be surprised!"

Marc grinned at her. "I thought you liked to travel fast."

"I do—but not on a night like this at the risk of life and limb. Besides, I'm mad at you. What's the idea of asking me to dinner and then spending the evening arguing with that man about a dead cow?"

"Paragraph two, page eighteen, section C, land grant charter for the C. H. R. R., reads—and I quote—'Be it herein enacted that the party of the second part (that's us), its agents or assigns, shall in perpetuity, install and maintain adequate fence protection bordering its right of way, and shall assume responsibility for damage to any and all livestock due to inadequacy of said protection,' end quote. 'That man' had a cow hit on the tracks. He says our fence was down and threatens to sue us. With Archie away, I had to investigate. Part of my job, remember?"

"Well, you didn't have to spoil my evening doing it," pouted Nora. "Why don't you quit this railroad foolishness? You worked so hard to get your degree, and now you waste time seeing people about dead cows!"

"There'd be people to see about dead cows in any law practice. Things move on a railroad, and I don't mean just trains. Something's likely to pop any time. About a week of writing wills and checking deeds, and I'd be picking daisies out of the air. Railroading's in my blood, Nora, just as it's in your father's. Which reminds me—I want to see the old gent. Let's head for the tower."

"You two!" said Nora bitterly. "Neither one of you has a drop of blood. Just steam and cinders!"

They rode in silence for several miles, until Marc slowed for an intersection, and turned onto a narrow dirt road. It wound through a dense thicket and crossed a network of railroad tracks. After negotiating a series of bumpy crossings, Marc stopped beside a lonely building set in the middle of the maze. The four sides, on the second floor, were enclosed in glass, and a faint light shone on the haze that covered the switch yard.

Marc and Nora climbed the steep, narrow steps that angled up one side of the building to the tower. Stepping into the dimly lit room, Nora blew a kiss toward the man seated at the control board.

"Hello, Dad," she said.

"Hi kids. How's everything?" replied O'Conner, twisting around in his chair and grinning at them.

"Fine, Dad, only do you know what this string bean did? He asked me to dinner at Rosedale Inn, that new place outside town. Why? So that he could whisper sweet words to me across a table for two? No! Because he wanted to see the owner about a cow killed on the tracks last week! The nerve!"

"That's not fair, Nora," retorted Marc. "I did whisper sweet words to you. Besides, the expense account carries the dinner."

"Marry him, Nora. Combine business and pleasure."

"Marry a railroader? Not me. I want my husband home nights. When he gets tired of playing train—well—" She flushed and shot a quick glance at Marc.

"Marc told me you two could never get along. You're too stubborn," chuckled O'Conner.

Marc dropped into a dilapidated chair, standard equipment in any signal tower, and cocked a heel against the rim of the stove.

"How's the railroad, Johnny?" he asked.

"Good shape so far," replied O'Conner, casting a critical eye over the board, "except for that darn hoghead draggin' the dog. Erratic. Had him figured for twenty-two minutes Zackery to Moosehead, and he done it in sixteen flat. Can't figure that feller."

"The dog?" questioned Marc with a puzzled frown.

"Yeah. The local. Stops at every lamp post!"

Marc chuckled. "Oh, I see."

O'Conner suddenly slapped the heel of his hand against his forehead and spun around to the machine.

"Holy gee!" he exclaimed. "Forgot Number 6. Whole fool railroad'll be standin' still!"

He rapidly twisted the knobs on his telephone switchboard to call the station operators.

An excited voice burst out of the loudspeaker. "Hello, ZA!"

"Shut up!" barked O'Conner. "Got a 19 comin'. Wait'll I'm done."

"Lowell."

"Marquette."

"Delton."

One by one the station operators identified themselves.

"Okay, you fellers," said O'Conner, speaking slowly and distinctly in spite of his need for haste. "All of you make a 19—better make about seven copies." He studied the train sheet, and carefully spelled out the order—a meet between Number 6 and Number 13. When he had finished, the operators rapidly read back the order, one by one. As each finished, O'Conner checked his book and recorded the time. When the last one was through he flipped a switch on the board and spoke again into the telephone.

"All right, who wants the dispatcher?"

"Johnny," replied the excited voice. "Morrison. I'm at Zola. I just got derailed!"

"Well, what'm I s'pposed to do? You crazy apes run your motorcars like to a fire. You'll get a week fer bein' careless."

"No sir, Johnny. I'm followin' 61 in and eased across the crossing careful like. I wasn't doin' ten miles a hour or I'da been killed. Know what pitched me?"

"What's this," snapped O'Conner in exasperation, "a game o' riddles?"

"A hand axe!"

"A hand axe?"

"Yeah. Musta been layin' in the crossin'."

"What the devil was a hand axe doin' there?"

"I dunno. Fell off a the train, I guess. Funny thing— the head's covered with blood!"

"Blood!" exclaimed Marc, his body stiffening with interest.

"Blood!" said O'Conner. "Morrie, you kiddin'?"

"No, I ain't kiddin'. Looks fishy to me, so I called ya."

"You don't suppose—" muttered Marc thoughtfully.

"Oh—it couldn't be! Zola—that crossing about thirty miles from here?"

"Yeah."

"Quite a run on a motorcar at night. Tell Morrison to take the axe with him. Someone may ask for it."

"Morrie, take that axe with you. Bring it along next time you come in. Go easy, now."

"Okay, Johnny."

O'Conner cut his switch and turned to find Nora watching him with excited eyes.

"How do you suppose that axe got there?" she asked.

"Oh, lots of people walk the tracks, and this is hunting season," drawled Marc. "Probably some hunter dropped it. . . . Number 61—that's the Chicago Flyer, isn't it, Johnny?"

"Yeah. Been nursin' him all evenin'. He's draggin' Mr. Richards' car."

"That means your vacation is over, Marc. The boss's coming home," teased Nora.

"No, not yet," said O'Conner. He ain't figurin' on stoppin' here. The car's billed through to Chicago."

"Let's see, he's about due." Marc glanced at the clock.

"Yeah—11:45. There, he's on the approach now. Right on the button."

"Guess I'll walk over and watch him come in," said Marc, starting for the door. "Might get a chance to say hello to old Dick."

"Me too," cried Nora, tripping along behind him.

They clattered down the steep steps.

"Do I recall someone of my acquaintance making derogatory remarks about railroading?" asked Marc.

"All right, stupid, get going," said Nora, pushing him gently.

They scrambled across the tracks as the big engine panted to a halt opposite the station. Nora, unsteady in high heels, picked her way gingerly over the slippery ties.

Floodlights, hung in the sky at the top of slender poles, shed an eerie half-light over the switch yard, and reflected in thin streaks of silver from the rails. A tiny speck of light danced up and down at the far end of the yard where a brakeman signaled the engineer in the cab of a mile-long freight train. Another light, bobbing and ducking under the passenger train, traced the course of a "car knocker" checking the brakes and wheel bearings. The "puff-swish-puff" of a pneumatic greasing machine, busily lubricating the engine, played an accompaniment to the shouts and thumps of baggage handlers loading baggage and mail.

Marc and Nora stepped onto the platform at the rear of the train. Passengers were disembarking from several points, and others waited their turn to board. A man in a conductor's cap and blue coat leaped from the forward step of the last car and started for the station at a run. He reached the door of the station as Marc rounded the end of the train.

"Hello, Holland!" called Marc. The man turned and trotted back.

"Good grief, Mr. Jordan! Am I glad to see you! We got trouble."

"What's the matter, Holland?"

"Look," he replied, leading the way to the steps between the last two cars. Nora, starting up after Marc, found him rooted to the step, staring at the platform. She tried to see past him, but his flapping coat tails blinded her.

"What's the matter, Marc? What is it?"

He turned slowly, his face pale and drawn in the dim light. "Listen carefully, Nora. Go back to the tower and tell your father to run this train onto a siding. Now! It'll be here a while. Tell him I'll take the rap for the delay. Call Inspector Jerry Anderson at police headquarters. If he isn't there, call him at home. Stay on the phone until you get him. Tell him to get here on the double. Then ask Johnny to call Morrison and have him bring in the axe he found. Tell him to forget about twenty-mile speed limits, and wheel that motorcar. Hurry!"

"But, Marc—"

"I said hurry. Beat it! And stay in the tower until I come back for you."

He turned back to a white-faced Holland who was clutching the hand rail and staring unsteadily at the crumpled figure on the platform.

"Not very pretty, is it? Who discovered this, Holland?"

"Cliff, Mr. Richards' porter. He come to me scared to death. Says Mr. Richards had his head cut off. He could hardly talk. I thought he was crazy, but, by golly, he was darn near right!"

"Who else knows about it?"

"Nobody. We just found him ten minutes ago. I figured the best thing was to run in fer help. I stayed on the platform."

"You shouldn't have let the passengers unload," said Marc severely. "The murderer has very likely stepped off the train and disappeared."

"Good gosh, never thoughta that, Mr. Jordan. This kinda hit me in the middle. Guess I wasn't thinkin' very good."

"Well, it's too late now, and you did your best. Not many people have to face a mess like this. Have you touched anything?"

"Not me!" exclaimed Holland with fervor. "I just stood by the door and held my belly down!"

"Yes, I see what you mean. How's the train made up?"

"There's Mr. Richards' car, two Pullmans, three coaches, a mail car, express car, and two baggage cars."

"How about your crew? Can you account for them? Who's carrying the flag?"

"None of 'em been back here except Adams. He's flaggin'. Here he is now," Holland replied as a man came up to the step.

"What's the hold-up, Holland?" asked Adams. "Ye gods!" he gasped, staring at the figure on the platform.

"Adams, have you been back here this evening?" asked Marc.

"No sir—I mean—yes sir," stuttered Adams. "Dropped off to flag at Hastings."

"See anything unusual?"

"No sir."

"Was anyone hanging around the rear of the train?"

"No sir."

"Did you notice what was going on in the private car?"

"It was all lit up. Four guys was playing cards, and the porter was servin' drinks, or something."

"Who's on the car?" asked Marc, turning to Holland.

Holland thought a moment. "Mr. Richards, his secretary, his daughter and her husband, Mr. Johnson, and Mr. Linden."

"See any of them before you left?"

"Just Mr. Richards. He always comes up to kid the crew."

"Did he seem like himself?"

"Same as always. Great guy, he was. I was brakin' the first train he fired on, thirty-six years ago. What a way fer a guy like him to kick off," he added sadly.

Marc grimaced. "I doubt that anyone would choose such a mode of departure. I wonder who could have hated him enough for that. Here come your siding orders," he said as a door to the station slammed and a man started toward the train. "Take care of that, Holland. Then check with your crew on the coach passengers. See how many got off the train, and if you can identify any of them. Adams, find the Pullman conductor. I want him to check his list.

I want to know if anyone got off here. And give me your lantern. I'll need some light to look around."

As the others went off on their errands, Marc flashed the lantern around the grisly platform. The body of Richards lay crumped against the far door, his right arm doubled under his body and his feet sprawled out partly obstructing the door. His head was jammed into the corner formed by the outside door and the corner of the car partition. A gash had been cut from his left shoulder, at the base of the neck, into his back. Marc's mouth twitched as the light probed the details of the wound. Someone had meant to kill the man, and no mistake. The light coat was saturated with blood. Blood was splattered over the door and wall. A puddle had formed in the corner and extinguished a big black cigar. A line of blood drops made an arc along the runway to the platform of the forward car. Marc gingerly touched his finger to some of the blood. It was still sticky. He carefully examined the windows, the door and door handles, and the catches on the outside.

Distastefully wiping the blood from his hand, he quietly opened the door into the private car.

4

Marc stepped into the passage at the end of the car. The aisle was dimly lit by shaded night lights, with a soft glow at the far end from lamps in the lounge. The car was quiet with the muffled silence of soft carpets and heavy steel. All the stateroom doors were closed except the first, which led to the porter's berth and galley. Two round, terrified eyes stared at him from a dark shadow of a face perched above a white coat.

"Who is yo'?" asked a quavering Southern voice.

"Hello, Cliff. Marc Jordan. Don't you remember me?"

"Oh, Lawdy, Lawdy, Mistah Jawd'n. All's seen ghosts tonight! Ah bin so scairt de debbil was comin' fo' me sho'."

"Take it easy, Cliff," said Marc soothingly. "Nothing to be afraid of. When did you find Mr. Richards?"

"Ah don' know jist when it was, Mistah Jawd'n. Ah bin up fo'wud passin' de time o' day wid Andrews, de po'tah in de nex' cah. Ah was comin' back to see was evabody in bed so's to kinda clean up, an' dere he was, blood all ovah evah place. Like to scairt me to death. Ah runs right up front an' gits Mistah Holland."

"See anyone around this part of the train?"

"No suh, nobody 'cept some o' de passengers up front."

"But no one around this platform?"

"No suh."

"How did you happen to be off the car? Aren't you supposed to be on duty all the time?"

"Well, Miss Joan an' Miss Ahthuh done gone to bed befo', an' Mistah Richahds an' Mistah Linden, dey was goin', so Mistah Richahds say Ah cud go too. He always say dat, but Ah nevah does. Ah always stays aroun' till dey is all in bed, to clean up. So Ah slipped up to see Andrews. Mistah Richahds say Ah was through," he added defensively, regaining some of his composure.

"Where were you and Andrews?"

"Men's room, nex' cah fo'wahd."

"Which end of the car?"

"Dis end, suh."

"Did you see anyone go by while you were there?"

"Seems lak Ah did see de curtains swish lak somebody went by, but Ah cain't be sho'."

"When was that?"

"Ah don' remembah, Mistah Jawd'n. Ah wasn't payin' no 'tention."

"Who else is on this car besides Mr. Richards?"

"Well, dere's Miss Joan an' Mistah David, an' Mistah Johnson, an' Mistah Linden, an' Miss Ahthuh."

"Which rooms do they have?"

"De fust one off de lounge, dat's Miss Joan an' Mistah David's. Nex' is Mistah Richahds, nex' Mistah Johson, nex' Mistah Linden, 'nen Miss Ahthuh."

"Have you heard anything while you've been waiting?"

"No suh, ain't bin a soun', 'cept mah teeth rattlin'."

"Now, Cliff, I want to look around before the place gets messed up. You watch the platform. I don't want anyone to fool around there until the police arrive."

"Does Ah have to go out dere, Mistah Jawd'n? Ah cain't do it! Ah gits goose pimples jist thinkin' 'bout it."

"I don't blame you," said Marc, smiling wryly. "No, you don't have to go out. Stand by the door, and see that no one comes up. You won't have to look at Mr. Richards at all. And be quiet. I don't want to disturb the others yet."

"Yas suh, Mistah Jawd'n."

Marc walked slowly along the passageway and Cliff took up his post at the door. The train jerked gently, clicked across switch points, and moved onto a siding. He flashed his light along the carpet, the windows and window sills, the door panel. Then it darted back to a case mounted in the wall above the window halfway down the aisle. It was a case with a glass door containing wrecking tools: a long-handled fireman's axe; a crowbar; a jimmy; a flashlight; but what caught his eye and brought out a low whistle was a blank space in the case. A space which, judging by the mounting clips and the marks on the background board, had held a small hand axe! The glass door to the case was held by a snap catch and stood slightly ajar. Marc gingerly pulled the door open and examined the case carefully, flashing his light along the glass and into the corners.

After completing his examination of the aisle, Marc stepped into the lounge room and studied the beautiful furnishings. The room was enclosed by an expanse of glistening windows. A comfortable leather davenport partially filled one side under the windows. An overstuffed chair and lamp were fitted into each corner, and there was a mahogany writing desk against the forward partition. A bridge table was placed opposite the end of the davenport, surrounded by chairs at odd angles, and littered with cards. A large Pullman ash tray at the opposite end of the davenport was covered with smoking debris. Mare picked up one cigarette which had been lit and snuffed out immediately. He flashed his light along the floor, under the chairs and davenport where the shaded lights failed to penetrate, and thumbed through the miscellaneous papers and magazines on the writing desk.

Walking slowly through the lounge, he opened the door at the rear and stepped onto the observation platform. It was quite spacious. Several chairs were pushed into a group at one side. A railing completely surrounded the outer edge of the platform, and his light picked up the glistening sheen of polished chromium. The top of the car formed the roof, and a small awning under the edge gave additional protection against rain and sun. Marc leaned over the railing and examined the awning carefully, working around from one side to the other, clutching his coat to keep from touching the rail. Getting down on hands and knees, he examined the floor inch by inch. A ground out cigarette butt met his eye; a crumpled page from a timetable; several round black spots in one corner and near them a piece of lint hooked in a small rust snag. In the other corner his light picked out a stain where water had formed rivulets in the loose soot, and dried.

The wail of a police siren faded into silence at the station across the yard. Marc rose, brushing the dust from his clothes. Glancing up, he stepped into the lounge, strode to one of the doors, and knocked gently.

After a moment of silence, he rapped again. There was a faint rustle, followed by the click of a light switch.

"Yes, who is it?" called a clear voice.

"Marc Jordan, Miss Joan. May I speak to you, please?"

A few seconds later the door opened to disclose Joan clutching a robe around her shoulders. Her dark hair made an attractive, tousled halo around her white face, and her big eyes, misty with sleep, met Marc's wonderingly.

"Why, Marc, what in the world are you doing here?"

"Good evening, Miss Joan. My apologies for intruding at this hour."

"That's all right," replied Joan. "Are you going to Chicago with us? Daddy didn't mention it."

Marc shook his head. "No, I—I'm—could I speak to Mr. Arnold, please?"

Joan's eyes opened wide in surprise. "Why, yes, I guess so. David?" She turned from the door and called to her husband in the upper berth.

A rumpled head appeared over the edge, and a pair of sleepy eyes, full of annoyance, stared at Marc.

"Um-m. Huh? Oh, hello, Jordan. You pick a fine time to come to call!"

"Sorry, Dave. Will you step into the lounge, please? This is very important."

Joan's glance darted wonderingly from her husband to Marc. Arnold reared up in the berth grumpily.

"What the devil! Won't it keep till tomorrow?"

Marc shook his head. "I'm afraid not. Please hurry." He turned quickly and strode back to the lounge. He twirled a lock of hair round his finger for several seconds before he was joined by Arnold.

"What's up?" demanded Arnold.

Marc continued twirling the lock of hair.

"A mess, Dave." He hesitated and then said bluntly, "Miss Joan's father was murdered tonight!"

"What?" gasped Arnold. His face turned ashen. He swayed slightly and leaned against the arm of the davenport for support.

"Murdered," repeated Marc. "The police'll be here any moment, and Joan must know. I haven't the courage to tell her, so you'll have to do it."

"But how—"

"Never mind the details," interrupted Marc. "I'm sorry, but there isn't time. I don't know how you are going to break it to her gently, but it'll come better from you than from Anderson. He isn't gentle about anything."

"But, Marc—"

"Please, Dave," pleaded Marc. "Take my word for it, he's dead! Murdered! You comfort Mrs. Arnold the best you can."

Marc hurried away, leaving Arnold, shaken and horrified, standing in the lounge. He stepped gingerly over the obstruction on the platform and ran to meet the caravan coming across the yard.

The group was led by a short, stocky man. His bare, bald head glistened in the yard light, and sharp eyes, magnified by thick lenses, peered through horn-rimmed spectacles. He was followed by a man carrying a small case, another with tripod and camera over his shoulder, and several burly policemen. Tagging along behind came Nora, skirts flying, clutching her hat and dancing daintily over the tracks. Marc headed them off a short distance from the train.

"Howdy, Jordan," said the bald-headed man. "Miss O'Conner said you were here. What's up?"

"Hello, Jerry. You made it in a hurry," replied Marc. "Bad business. Murder!"

"You don't say," said Anderson dryly. "Miss O'Conner hinted at it, so I brought the boys along—just in case. Well, where's the corpse, and who is it?"

"On the platform," said Marc, pointing to the private car. "Allow me to present Mr. Richards, president of the railroad!"

"Whew," whistled Anderson. "Brother, you've got trouble. That's bad. I don't like fancy murders. Too much publicity. Well, let's get going. What do you know about it?" he asked as they hurried toward the car.

"Nothing," replied Marc. "Nothing that won't keep. You fellows had better get to work. We've held this train twenty minutes, and several hundred people are going to start raising the roof. Say!" he exclaimed, turning suddenly to Nora. "Didn't I ask you to stay in the tower?"

"Who do you think you are, Marc Jordan, to order me around!" she replied indignantly. "Do you think I'd miss this fun?"

"Fun? All right, if you call it that," grumbled Marc. "But it won't be pleasant. What do you think of that, Jerry?" he asked, pointing to the platform.

"Great day!" exclaimed Anderson. "Look at that! Somebody really meant business, and no fooling. Looks like he'd been hit with a meat cleaver. Any trace of the weapon?"

"That's strange, Jerry," replied Marc. "It seems we found the weapon before we knew there'd been a murder."

"Huh? How come?"

"Morrison, signal maintainer, was out on trouble tonight, and followed this train in on his motorcar. At Zola he hit something. Derailed. He found an axe, covered with blood, in the crossing."

"Well, I'll be damned! There's a break. On the track, eh? Could've dropped off the train, then."

"Yes," replied Marc. "It's obvious how the job was done. Richards was standing on the platform, looking out of the window. Just lit a cigar. He was struck from behind on the left. The murderer stepped through to the next car—see the line of blood drops?—opened the car door, dropped the axe out."

"Yup, quick and convenient."

"I'll wager this's the first time you've found the weapon before the corpse, Jerry," continued Marc. "I'll wager further that the axe was taken from a case of tools in Mr. Richards' own car. One is missing."

"Well," said Anderson, "that makes it easy. Open and shut. We find who could get the axe, and there's our man. Nothing to it."

"Not so fast," cautioned Marc. "Anyone could slip back from the front part of the train and get the axe. Quite a lot of passengers got off here. Could've been any of them."

"The devil they did! Then our bird has flown. What's the matter with the conductor? How come he let 'em off?"

"You can't blame Holland. Cliff, Mr. Richards' porter, found him just before the train pulled in. Holland was so excited he didn't think about holding the passengers. By the time I got here it was too late."

"Hm," muttered Anderson. "Well, let's get to work, boys. Joe, I want a lot of good pictures. Get him from all angles. And, Doc, look him over and see what you make of it. Sergeant," he continued, turning to one of the officers, "go over to the station and call headquarters. Have 'em send out a wagon. Tell the desk man to get Murphy out here with his fingerprint stuff. Now, how about these people on the train? Talked to any of 'em, Jordan?"

"Just to Richards' daughter and her husband. I thought it a good idea to prepare them. Haven't heard from the others yet. No one else on the train knows anything is wrong. We've been keeping everyone off the platform."

"What shall we do with the passengers? We can't hold 'em all, and it'll take all night to grill 'em, one at a time."

"Right. The Pullman conductor is checking his list, and maybe he can help us. Here he is now."

"Mr. Jordan," said the Pullman conductor, coming up with his car sheets in his hand, "all Pullman passengers are aboard except five. Three of 'em, an old couple and a young feller, had space to Calumet. One man on this car," he indicated the last Pullman, "had through space. He told the porter not to make up his berth, and got off here. A woman in the next car pulled the same stunt, only her berth was made up. Them two look fishy."

"Any description?" asked Anderson.

"Not much," replied the conductor. "The old folks seemed like plain people, and I don't remember the young man. The other two I never saw. Porter took their tickets."

"Could he describe 'em?"

"Well, he says the man was tall, heavy-set, fat in the face, and had on a light gray suit. The woman was medium size, had on a tan coat, dark glasses and a scarf on her head."

"Hm. Not much. How about coach passengers?"

"Holland handles them. You'll have to ask him."

"I been checking, Mr. Jordan," said Holland, joining the group. "A coupla dozen got off, but the boys can't tell a thing about 'em. We never pay much attention to passengers' looks."

"Jerry," interrupted Marc, "why not detail a couple of men to run down these passengers, and a couple more to check through the train."

"Good idea, Jordan. Meyers, you and George work out of the station. Get the description of those two? All right, work on them first. Check taxi drivers and red caps. Follow up any leads. If you get stuck, call headquarters for more men. You other fellows work through the train. The conductors will help. Take the name of anyone who knows anything. Check to see if any coach passengers came back through the Pullman cars. Make it snappy. How're we doing, Doc?" he asked as the doctor came down the steps, whistling softly.

"Well, Anderson," replied the doctor, "it is my considered opinion that the man is dead— very dead. Don't ask me was he poisoned, or drowned, or strangled, because he wasn't. He was hit, presumably hard, on the left shoulder with an instrument presumably heavy, but sharp, and his head was darn near cut off! Going to be a nice scrubbing job there for someone," he added, eyeing the splattered blood with admiration.

"How long's he been dead?"

"Oh, can't say exactly. Not very long. Anywhere from fifteen minutes to an hour."

"Hold it a minute," interrupted Marc abruptly. The putt-putt of a motorcar died away on the next track, and a man hopped off. "Here's Morrison with the axe. Nice work, Morrie; just in time. Would that do it, Doc?" he asked, pointing to the axe Morrison held gingerly between thumb and finger.

The doctor examined the blood-caked head and handle critically.

"Let's see," he said. "About five inches across the blade. Not too heavy, but heavy enough. Yes, I'd say that would do very nicely."

"By the way, Doctor," said Marc quietly, "could a woman have used that axe?"

"A woman? Sure. A child could swing an axe like that and kill a man."

"There's Exhibit 'A,' Jerry."

"Darned if it ain't. Here, Martin, take care of this." He handed the axe to one of the men. "Go easy on it. Don't want to spoil the evidence any more than it is already. When Murphy gets here, have him fingerprint it. Tell him to go over the platform, too, and then to stick around. He'll have work inside. When the wagon gets here, take this away." He pointed to Richards' body. "It's no good for anything but daisy fertilizer now. You know, it's a funny thing. Don't matter who a man is—when he's a corpse, he's a corpse. I can't understand how those people can be so quiet in there."

"Passengers usually stay in bed, once they get there," replied Marc. "They chalk delays up to railroad inefficiency."

"Well, let's get 'em up. Looks like we're gonna be here all night." He climbed into the car, followed by Marc and Nora.

5

"Cliff," said Marc, as the porter held the door for them, "get Mr. Linden and Mr. Johnson and tell them to come into the lounge. Also Miss Arthur and Mr. Arnold. There's no use to upset Miss Joan, so ask her to stay in her room. You stay with her."

"Yas suh, Mistah Jawd'n," replied Cliff.

"Come on, Jerry," Marc continued; "you'll want to look the car over. That's where the axe came from." He pointed to the case of tools.

"How very handy," muttered Anderson. "A man could really pick his weapon outa there. I thought these cases had locks on 'em. How come this one has a catch?"

"This's a private car," replied Marc. "They probably put a catch on it for convenience."

"Convenience of the murderer, I'd say," said Anderson sourly. "Lord, what a dump!" he exclaimed as they moved into the lounge. "Can't figure out why I took up policing. Looks like being a railroad president has a lot more future. I'll bet he never bought that davenport at no auction!"

"Well, Jerry, this railroad president doesn't have much future, at the moment," said Marc dryly.

"You got me there, all right. . . . Well, now, a party." He pointed to the collection of glasses. Then, muttering to himself, he worked around the room. "Papers on the

39

desk; nothing funny there. Ash tray full of butts—they always are—bonded stuff, I'd say." He sniffed one of the glasses. "Nothing under the davenport, or the cushions. Cards look like the bid was made, so that couldn't be the motive! Looks on the level, Jordan. What's out there?" He pointed to the rear door.

"Observation platform. There's nothing out there either, but you'd better look it over."

Anderson stepped through the door and played his flashlight around the platform briefly.

"Someone could get into the car from the roof," he said thoughtfully.

"Not likely," argued Marc. "That'd be doing it the hard way. It'd take a clever acrobat to get up or down over that smooth, curved roof and awning. I looked it over, and don't think anyone did."

"Guess you're right," agreed Anderson. "Where the heck are those guys? We ain't got all night!"

"They'll be along. Here's one now. Mr. Arnold, Inspector Anderson. Arnold's Mr. Richards' son-in-law."

Arnold was dressed but had forgotten to comb his hair. His neat suit, shining shoes and tousled head made an odd contrast. His face was pale and composed, except that the lobes of his nostrils twitched spasmodically. Anderson eyed him suspiciously.

"What d'you know about this, Arnold?" he asked.

Arnold shook his head. "Nothing," he said flatly. "Marc just told me about it a few minutes ago."

"Zat so? Humph! We'll see about that. . . . Where you guys been?" he demanded impatiently of the two startled, flustered men who came through the door. "Wanta keep us here all night? Introduce me, Jordan."

"Mr. Johnson, president of Calumet National Bank," said Marc, pointing toward Johnson, "and Mr. Linden, secretary-treasurer of the railroad. Inspector Anderson."

Eric Linden furtively darted pale eyes from face to face. A nervous hand alternately stroked his chin and smoothed his rumpled hair.

"What's this about Richards? What's Cliff mumbling about?" demanded Johnson.

"Yes, for pity sakes, what is the matter?" stammered Linden.

"Come in, Miss Arthur," interrupted Marc quietly.

Anderson turned to stare at the woman standing in the doorway. Her hair hung down her back in two braids, and she clutched a bright-colored housecoat at her throat. Dark shadows rimmed her eyes, and she steadied herself with a trembling hand on the door case.

"What is it?" she whispered. "Why was I wakened?"

"Have a seat, ma'am," said Anderson. He whirled on the two men.

"You fellows sit down and shut up!" he said roughly. "If you don't know already," he looked around at each of them meaningly, "Mr. Richards was murdered a little while ago! Now sit down!"

"Murdered!" gasped Linden.

Miss Arthur collapsed into a chair in the corner. Her housecoat dropped open unheeded, disclosing a frilly, revealing nightgown. She dropped her head in both hands and whimpered softly.

Marc watched, his eyes darting from face to face.

Johnson seated himself in one of the big chairs and fished a gold cigarette case out of the pocket of his bathrobe. Calmly selecting a cigarette, he tapped it against the case and lit it with a flick of a fighter. Inhaling deeply, he returned Anderson's stare.

Linden squatted on the edge of a chair opposite Johnson. He clutched his robe around him and shivered.

Marc offered a pack of cigarettes, first to Arnold who shook his head, and then to Linden who nervously fumbled for one. He dropped it on the floor and broke a match before he succeeded in getting a light.

While Anderson fussed with a notebook and cleared a space at the desk, Marc stepped to the door of Arnold's room and knocked gently. Cliff opened the door, and Marc saw Joan, fully dressed, sitting rigidly on the berth staring into space.

"Oh, Marc, it's so horrible! What am I to do?"

"I'm terribly sorry, but there isn't much you can do. Inspector Anderson is getting the story from the others, but it won't be necessary to bother you now. You can't go to Chicago. Why don't you have Cliff call for your car, and go home?"

Joan nodded dumbly.

"See to it, Cliff. We'll call you, Miss Joan, if we need you."

Slowly Joan's eyes raised to his. Slowly they filled with tears.

"He's dead!" she whispered. "Daddy's dead! Murdered!" Her voice rose shrilly. "Oh, it's horrible!" She hunched forward and let her head fall in her lap. Great sobs twisted her body.

Marc laid a clumsy hand on her shoulder. "Please, Miss Joan," he said unsteadily, "that won't help. I'm very sorry."

Joan straightened up. Tight fists now lay in her lap, and a jerky sigh whistled through her clenched teeth.

"I know it, Marc," she mumbled. "I'll be all right."

As Cliff hurried out on his errand, Marc closed the door, and stepped quickly into what had been Mr. Richards' room. The lights were on, and a pair of blue silk pajamas were draped across the freshly made berth. A traveling case lay open on a stand, with shirts and underclothes neatly arranged. Marc pawed through the case, looked under the berth. He glanced through the door to a tiny lavatory. Opening the door to a medicine closet, he found a neat array of shaving equipment.

He repeated the process in the room beyond. This one was smaller. The berth was tumbled, and a suit and underclothes were dumped carelessly over a chair. Marc swept his flashlight under the berth. It flicked to a wadded rag stuffed in one corner. Shaking it out gingerly, he saw that it was a Pullman hand towel, streaked and splotched with blood. He thoughtfully put the towel back under the berth and continued his search. As he lifted a wastebasket under the washstand, he saw a crumpled piece of ordinary writing paper. Carefully untangling the folds, a note in fine backhand met his eye:

Dicky—Meet me stateroom 'A,' next car, at 11:30.

No signature or identification. Marc examined a collection of loose dirt in the pocket formed by the crushed paper. Then, taking out his handkerchief, he wrapped the ball of paper in it, and slipped it into his pocket.

He went to the next room, Linden's. This was a duplicate of the other except that the bed was turned neatly back, a light suit was hung carefully on a hanger and underwear folded on a chair.

"One of those fellows!" muttered Marc.

Miss Arthur's door stood open. A pair of stockings were draped on a hook over the lavatory.

Underclothes were laid over the top of a small traveling case which stood open on a chair. Marc quickly felt through the case, then stepped back into the aisle.

Finished with his hurried reconnaissance, Marc returned to the lounge and dropped into a chair beside Nora, whose eyes, bright with excitement, met his questioningly. He gave her a slow wink, stretched his legs into the middle of the car and, tilting his hat over his eyes, studied the tense faces.

"All right now," said Anderson sharply. "I want a complete story of what went on here tonight. Don't leave anything out. Let's start with you, Mr. Johnson. When did you get on the car—and where?"

"A little after seven this evening, at the siding about thirty miles from Duck Lake. That's where Richards keeps—or rather kept—this car when he was there."

"Where were you before that?"

"At my summer home on Duck Lake. Mrs. Johson and I have been having a vacation."

"You got to the car—how?"

"We all went together, all except Linden. Richards' summer home's next to mine. He drove us to the train in a station wagon he keeps—kept—there."

"And you, Linden?"

"I was in St. Paul on business. I rode the train, and transferred when the car was picked up at the siding."

"What were you doing in St. Paul—company business?"

"Yes—partly."

"Partly?"

"Well, I attended to some private banking business—if you must know!" Linden said defiantly.

"I must know—and will know—everything, my friend," snapped Anderson. "So you all got together around seven-thirty. Then what?"

"We had dinner. That was the arrangement. Cliff's an excellent cook," replied Johnson. His slender fingers curved carelessly around his cigarette and he flipped the ash in the general direction of a wastebasket.

Anderson turned to Arnold. "Where were you before you got on the train?"

"Joan and I were at the cottage at Duck Lake. Joan is Mr. Richards' daughter, you know, and we were staying with him."

"You ate. How long'd that take?"

"We were through about eight-thirty or a quarter to nine, I think," said Johnson.

"Talk about anything in particular?"

"Don't think so. Richards was bragging about a fish he'd caught. Other than that I don't remember. We played some bridge. Mrs. Arnold and Miss Arthur went to bed quite early. Richards and Linden went about a quarter to eleven, and Arnold and I perhaps half an hour later. Isn't that right?" Johnson turned to Arnold. "And that covers it."

"Not quite!" said Anderson dryly. "When did Mrs. Arnold leave you?" he asked, turning to Arnold.

"About nine-thirty. A few minutes after we started to play bridge."

"Play bridge all evening?"

"Oh, no, we were all up and down," replied Johnson. "I went out on the platform once or twice. So did Arnold. Richards got up for drinks several times."

"Was Richards himself? I mean, anything funny about his actions?"

"No," said Johnson. "He was quite cheerful, in fact."

"I thought he spent a lot of time dreaming about something," remarked Arnold.

"He was to give a talk at the Railroad Club tomorrow," explained Linden, rubbing the side of his nose nervously. "Probably had that on his mind."

"Okay," continued Anderson. "The bridge game broke up when?"

"Quarter to eleven," said Linden.

"Did you and Richards go right to bed?"

"Yes—we went into our rooms at the same time."

"Richards obviously didn't go to bed. Did you?" Anderson glared at Linden,

"Yes, I did," replied Linden, pulling his dressing gown around him as though he felt a draft. "I went right to bed and to sleep. I was very tired."

"Bet you were! And did you leave your room?"

"No!"

"You others"—Anderson turned to Johnson and Arnold —"did you go to bed at the same time?"

"No," replied Johnson. "I read a while, and Arnold went out on the platform for a smoke. When he came back we talked a few minutes, and he went to bed. I remember looking at my watch."

"What time would that have been?" interrupted Marc casually.

"Seven minutes after eleven," replied Johnson.

Anderson studied Johnson, his eyes blank and unwinking.

"Let's get this straight, Johnson," he said flatly. "By your own admission, you were the last one to leave the lounge, and were here after the others had all gone. Correct?"

Johnson leaned forward stiffly, his face ashen.

"Now look here—someone had to be the last one to go to bed. It happened to be me. That doesn't give you any right to make accusations!"

Anderson darted a glance at Marc, who was slowly shaking his head.

"No accusations, Mr. Johnson. Just a point to remember." Anderson turned to Arnold. "And you, Mr. Arnold, when you left Johnson, did you go directly to your room?"

"Yes, I did," nodded Arnold.

"Did you leave it again?"

"No. My wife can verify that."

"Johnson," interrupted Marc, "didn't you work on the railroad some years ago?"

Johnson looked at him in surprise. "Why, yes, I did. I worked as a signal helper out of Calumet. Why?"

"A railroader from 'way back," murmured Marc. "Interesting. Oh, no connection. I'm just curious."

"Jordan, let me run this, will you?" growled Anderson. "Mr. Johnson, after you left here—alone—what did you do?"

"I read for a few minutes and then went to bed. I must have gone right to sleep, because I didn't hear another thing until Cliff called me." Anderson's chin sank into his ample chest and he stared glumly at the floor.

"Strikes me funny you folks knew exactly what time it was all evening," he said.

"Not at all," replied Marc. "These are railroaders. Every railroad man lives by the tick of his watch. Most natural thing in the world for one of them to check the time about every third breath."

"Okay," sighed Anderson as the others nodded assent. "Looks to me like any of you had plenty of chance to sock Richards."

Marc pushed himself to his feet and strode to the door of Arnold's room. He opened the door in response to the faint "Come in!" following his knock. Joan was seated as he had left her. Her blank eyes met his questioningly.

"Miss Joan," said Marc, "could you help us clear up a point? Do you remember what time your husband came to bed?"

She pressed a hot palm to her forehead and thought a minute.

"Yes, I do," she said. "I recall trying to look at my watch, and then remembering that it is being repaired. I looked at my bed clock." She pointed to a tiny boudoir clock. "It was six or seven minutes after eleven. Is it important?"

"Could be," he replied. "Did he stay with you the rest of the evening?"

"Yes. Neither of us left the room."

"May I borrow your clock, please?" he asked. At her nod of assent, he took the clock and stepped back into the lounge.

"What time is it, Johnson?"

"It's twelve forty-two," said Johnson, pulling out his watch. Marc glanced at the clock in his hand, returned it to Joan, and settled back into his chair.

"What's eatin' you, Jordan?" Anderson asked impatiently.

"Well," drawled Marc, "Mrs. Arnold says that her husband came to bed six or seven minutes after eleven, and didn't leave the stateroom. Her clock and Johnson's watch check. Unimportant, of course."

Anderson glanced up quickly. "Oh, I get it!"

A sigh whistled through Arnold's puckered lips, and Marc flashed him a look of reassurance.

"Jerry, we can't hold this train forever. Let these people get dressed and go home. We can take a look through the train, and get rid of it. We're not going to learn much here tonight."

"All right, Jordan, but I'm going to hold this car."

"Of course. You should. I've sent for Mrs. Arnold's auto. They can all go home in that."

"Okay. You folks get dressed and beat it. But I'm warning you—don't anybody leave town without me knowing it. I want you where I can lay a finger on you."

He leaned back as the quartet shuffled out, and rubbed his bald head, his face a mask of perplexity.

"What d'you make of it, Jordan?"

"I'd say you don't have a thing yet. Arnold's the only one with a semblance of an alibi. As matters stand, any of the others could have done it—even Mrs. Arnold."

"You don't suspect her!" exclaimed Anderson.

"No," replied Marc, "I don't believe she could have faked her grief. Nor would I be inclined to suspect Cliff. He's been Mr. Richards' porter for years, and faithful as a dog. Of course you can't overlook him. That leaves Johnson, Linden, Miss Arthur, and a couple of hundred other people on the train!"

"Yes—damn it!" growled Anderson. "That's going to make it tough. Well, let's see those conductors, and take a look at the next car."

The ambulance squad was loading Richards' mortal remains onto a stretcher when they came out on the platform. Anderson called to a man idling beside the train, watching the operation disinterestedly.

"Murphy, how'd you make out on prints?"

"Lots, Chief. Usual stuff. Got a good one off that window." Murphy pointed to the glass in the door to the forward car. "Woman's left hand. Nothin' on the door knobs. All smeared. Corpse prints in the hand rail."

"Beat it inside and get those people. Give the car a going over. Check around the tool case, and the axe Meyers has. Probably all messed up by that railroad feller. Do what you can with it. Come on, Jordan; let's see what goes on in here."

They hurried into the next car and found Adams, Holland, the Pullman conductor, and two policemen talking excitedly in the smoking room.

"What'd you find, boys?"

"Not much, Chief," one of the policemen replied. "An old lady in the next car says she seen a woman in dark glasses leave the washroom around eleven-fifteen, and head for this car. Didn't see her again, and don't know if she come out on the platform or not."

"Got the old lady's name?"

"Yup, we got it."

"Anyone in this car see her?"

"Nope."

"No one come back from the coaches, Chief," volunteered the other cop. "A bunch of sailors're settin' in the rear end of the last coach. Been there all the way. They swear no one come by 'em."

"Well, that's something. Narrows the field a little."

"Jerry, not much we can do here. Let's let the train go," said Marc.

"Damn it, Jordan," exclaimed Anderson, "you're more worried about delaying a train than catching a murderer! What's the idea?"

"That's not it, Jerry. I think we'll have the murderer when we know who wanted Richards dead. You'll never find that out staring at these cars!"

"Okay—okay," grumbled Anderson. "Go ahead, Holland. Get your darn train out of here! Trains—phooey!"

"Now, Jerry," Marc grinned at him as they moved toward the rear of the car. "Don't let it get you. A cool head, you know."

"Oh, shut up!"

Anderson, his hand on the door knob, was about to step onto the platform when Marc stopped in his tracks and stared at the drinking fountain.

"Jerry!" he exclaimed. "Now what the—look at that!" He pointed to the wastebasket under the drinking fountain faucet.

His face a study in bewilderment, Anderson carefully picked a knife from its partially concealed nest among the paper cups, holding it gingerly by the hilt between thumb and forefinger.

"A kitchen knife," he said slowly.

Marc took the knife from Anderson, avoiding any contact except with the edge of the hilt.

"A kitchen knife it seems to be," he said, "and a very good one. The handle's bone, and you don't often see a circular silver hilt on a kitchen knife. Notice the blade. It's thick along the back, but the cutting edge is convex ground. That makes it possible to get a very sharp edge. Wouldn't that be a beautiful stabbing instrument! Funny it should be lying ten feet from a freshly cut up corpse!"

Anderson retrieved the knife and, fishing a small magnifying glass out of his pocket, stepped under a light.

"This knife wasn't used for no recent murder," he said, peering through the glass. "It'd take boiling water and a brush to clean blood outa the crack around the hilt. It's clean as a whistle. So what?"

Marc shook his head. "Haven't the faintest idea. Maybe no connection whatever. Better treat it as a clue, though, until we know different."

"Yeah, I suppose so. Take it along, if you like."

Marc stepped into the washroom and wrapped the knife in a towel.

When the two men came out on the platform, Cliff and a liveried chauffeur were herding a woebegone group toward a waiting limousine.

"Remember, you guys, stick around," called Anderson.

"Come into the car, Jerry," said Marc. "There's something I want to show you."

Leading the way to the second room, he pointed to the wadded towel under the berth where he had left it. Anderson stared blankly.

"A bloody towel! Damn you, Jordan! Why didn't you tell me this sooner? Whose room's this?"

"Johnson's," replied Marc calmly. "I didn't tell you for two reasons: First, I was afraid you'd arrest him on the spot; second, I wanted to see if Johnson'd try to get rid of it when he came back to dress. The fact that he didn't touch it proves nothing, though. Maybe he suspected that one of us saw it. He might reason that it'd be better to play dumb, and leave it alone."

"Nuts!" moaned Anderson. "This's getting beyond me. Well, one more exhibit for the record. By golly, I'm going to sit in that davenport. Might never get another chance. What did you find, Murphy?" he asked, dropping wearily into the soft cushions.

"No prints on the case. Not many around the car. That porter's a bear with the polish. A coupla clean prints on the outside rail towards one end. The middle's clean like a mirror."

"Murphy, will you check this, please?" asked Marc, handing him the knife salvaged from the wastebasket.

"Sure," said Murphy cheerfully, unwinding the towel and starting to work with brush and dust.

"Jordan," muttered Anderson in a discouraged voice, "I've a hunch this's going to be a tough one."

"Don't know, Jerry," replied Marc. "We don't know much yet. We haven't the slightest idea about motives. Maybe we'll gain some ground there when we check Richards' past life. These people were keeping very mum about motive. Some of them are holding back—or lying—or both. Here's an interesting point: we can tell exactly when the murder was committed. When the train passed over the crossing at Zola, it made a record on a chart in the dispatcher's office. O'Conner can tell us—almost to the second—when that was. Since the axe was found at the crossing, that ties the time down pretty definitely. Might help a lot."

"Might, at that," said Anderson. "How does it do it?"

"I don't understand how the chart works," replied Marc, "but it comes in handy sometimes— in case of murder, for example."

"It's an idea. I'll see O'Conner about it." Anderson rose slowly. "Then to headquarters. Maybe the boys have turned up something on those passengers."

"Come on, Nora," said Marc with a grin. "This's where we get some rest, and our official friend goes to work. Keep the dogs barking, Jerry!"

"Oh, go to the devil!" growled Anderson. "It still strikes me as suspicious that Johnson could be so sure of the time. Eleven-seven. That's an odd figure."

Marc shook his head. "Ask any railroad man the time, Jerry, and he will give it to you—to the second. They live by the tick of the clock. Anyone who hangs around a railroad gets the habit. See you in the morning."

6

Whistling softly, Marc strode briskly into the railroad office. It was littered with the debris and smudged with the soot of decades. He hooked his hat on a coat rack and dropped into a chair beside Nora's desk.

"Morning, Nora. How're the Irish this morning?"

"I feel terrible, Marc. I hardly slept at all. I saw axes all night. Someone was always chasing me with one."

"Why, darling," Marc teased her, smiling at her, "no one would chase you—not with an axe!"

"Oh, Marc, isn't it awful! Last night it seemed exciting. But this morning it's just horrible. Look at those people." She pointed in disgust to several huddles. "Everyone is talking—talking! Poor Mr. Richards! He was such a fine man. Who could have done such a thing?"

"I wish I knew," said Marc fervently. "The boss in yet?"

"Mr. Barber? Yes, he came in just a few minutes ago. He's in his office."

"I'd better see him before he gets tied up," said Marc, striding to the door marked "J. B. Barber—Vice-President." He found Mr. Barber sitting behind a huge glass-top desk poring over the morning paper.

"Good morning, Marc," said Mr. Barber, glancing up. "I see you have your name in the paper. There's hardly any other news this morning."

"I was in at the kill last night—literally. It's a mess."

"Very mildly put," replied Barber. "It's a terrible blow to me. Dick Richards has been a real friend for many years. A fine man. He had faults—who doesn't?—but he ran this streak of rust with a firm hand. We're going to miss him."

"I know. The train men idolized him. He still went out once in a while and fired an engine all night—just for the fun of it, he said."

"Hope this chap Anderson's on the ball. You see, Marc, we don't know how much the company's involved. After all, Richards was our president. There's bound to be a lot of publicity, and I think we should keep a finger on the investigation."

Marc leaned forward eagerly. "I'd like to be that finger. That's one thing I came to see you about."

"Yes, you're better suited to it than I, though I'd like to work on it," said Barber wistfully, "if only to square things for old Dick. However, suppose you take charge in our interest. Now, tell me about it."

Marc gave him a brief outline of the happenings of the previous evening.

"There's one interesting angle. We know when the murder was committed—precisely."

"How's that?"

"The murder weapon—the hand axe from the tool case—was dropped at Zola Crossing, probably immediately after the murder. The signal equipment automatically recorded the time Number 61 passed the crossing, and in this case thereby recorded the time of murder."

"Hm," mused Barber. "Interesting. Fortunate the axe was found so soon. I see one of our men picked it up almost immediately."

"That's a break. I hope it's one the murderer didn't figure on. We really know practically nothing yet. The towel under his bed is perhaps embarrassing for Johnson. You've known these people for a long time. Is there any history that might give us a lead?"

"Well," replied Barber thoughtfully, rubbing a lean finger across the bridge of his nose, "I've known most of them for years. We grew up together. Both Johnson and Richards started the hard way, working on the railroad. They met head on over a girl, years ago, and Richards won out. Mrs. Richards died when Joan was born, and he never married again.

"Johnson got into real estate, and then into banking. Of late years, he and Richards have been quite friendly. Richards did his private banking at Calumet National, and they handled some of the railroad business."

"A love triangle twenty-five years ago's hardly grounds for murder. How about Linden?"

"A queer duck. Never married, and as far as I know has no interest in women. He lives alone in an apartment on Westchester. He collects old manuscripts; in fact he's a bit touched on the subject. He belongs to some organization of collectors and I've heard that he has paid terrific prices for some rare items. I've had a feeling that Richards had some hold on him, though I never knew what it was. Maybe I'm wrong. He annoyed Richards greatly at times, but old Dick wasn't one to hold a personal grudge against a man if he did his work. Linden is efficient."

"What do you think of Arnold?"

"Don't know him very well. He's brilliant. Came here from Chicago some years ago on an accounting assignment for the railroad, and wound up by marrying Joan. Richards didn't approve at the time. However, as it turned out, they got on fine. Arnold's a worker."

"Didn't Johnson marry a woman quite a bit younger than himself?"

"Have you met her?" asked Barber.

"No," replied Marc. "She's been pointed out to me, but our social circles don't intersect!"

"Look out," chuckled Barber. "She's a heartbreaker, if there ever was one. Even my dim old eyes can see that. She was an actress or dancer or something in Chicago. Rumor has it that Johnson saw her on the stage and took immediate steps!"

"How would you suggest that I approach this affair, sir?"

"I'll leave that to your judgment, Marc. Do what you can to protect the interest of the company. We're getting a big play in the papers. The longer it drags on, the worse it will be."

"We'll need to go through Mr. Richards' files and so forth. Any difficulty about that?"

"Needn't be," replied Barber. "You'd better be careful to work with the police. We don't want to be criticized for interference."

"Did Richards leave a will?"

"Yes. A very simple one. He left everything to his daughter. I prepared it for him several years ago. However," he added, "Richards requested that I prepare a new will a few weeks ago. Here it is." He extracted a document from his desk drawer. "He wanted it changed so that his property, except for his home and some cash, should be left in trust for Joan. In the event of her death it was to continue in trust for her children. If she had no children, or in the event of their death without heirs, all his property was to go to certain specified charities. This will was not signed, so the old one stands."

"Why did he want it changed?"

"He thought it made better provision for Joan, and took the responsibility for the management out of her hands."

"Thank you, Mr. Barber," said Marc, rising. "I'd better get to work. There's a lot to be done."

"Good luck, Marc. Keep me informed."

Marc picked his hat off the hook, blew a kiss toward Nora, and hurried out of the office. Running down the steps to the street, he hailed a cruising taxi and gave the address of police headquarters.

Arriving at the dingy stone building, he strolled up to the desk.

"Inspector Anderson in?" he asked.

"Yeah," replied the office on duty, "but he won't see ya. He's busy."

Marc chuckled. "I think he'll see me. Don't bother to announce me."

Mounting the worn wooden steps three at a time to a dim corridor on the second floor, he opened a door marked: "Homicide Squad—Inspector Anderson."

"Hey, what's the idea?" barked an angry voice. "Oh, hello, Jordan. Why don't you knock? What do you think this is, the aquarium?"

"Morning, Jerry," said Marc, sliding into a chair at the end of Anderson's desk. "You look terrible. Why don't you shave?"

"You wouldn't be so chipper yourself if you'd been up all night," growled Anderson.

Marc lit a cigarette. "Judging by the inspector's temper, I'd say things aren't going so well this morning."

"Going well!" snapped Anderson. "They ain't going— period. Confidentially, we haven't found a thing. Not a thing. I'd like to charge Johnson or Linden, or both of 'em, but I haven't got a bit of proof."

"I've just left Mr. Barber, Jerry. The railroad company's very much interested in this case—after all, Richards was our president. How about me working with you on it?"

"Now get this, Jordan," said Anderson, staring at Marc and beating square knuckles on the desk, "the police department investigates murders, and I'm in charge. I'll have nobody sticking their nose in and messing things up. You or nobody else."

"Wait a minute, Jerry," said Marc soothingly. "You don't understand. I'll just ride along. Maybe I can help a little. For instance, you'll want to go over Mr. Richards' private records. That's all fixed."

"Oh, well, that's different." Mollified, Anderson sank back in his chair. "Only I don't want any outside interference. I got trouble enough without worrying about some nitwit poking around."

"What've you found? Trace any of the passengers?"

"Yeah, some of 'em. The old folks are harmless. They're here visiting a son and his family. The guy that had Pullman space to Calumet's a chemist from St. Paul. Found him by checking the hotels. He's going to do research for a lumber mill. We checked them and he's okay. No trace yet of the lady in dark glasses. She's just disappeared. The boys're going through the cab drivers on a chance she maybe took a cab somewhere. Our fat-faced friend was picked up by a woman in a black sedan. One of the red caps saw him check a bag. Got a man at the check room, and when he comes for the bag, we'll get him."

"How about coach passengers?"

"No sale. We traced a few of 'em, but all dead ends. People who live here, or are visiting on legitimate business. Most of 'em we can't trace at all."

"Murphy dig up anything with his powder?"

"Nothing we didn't know last night," said Anderson with a discouraged sigh. "I sent him back this morning to check over the car again, but same thing. Fingerprints everywhere, but none that mean anything."

"Did you check the axe?"

"No prints. Say!" he exclaimed, leaning forward suddenly. "There's a funny thing. The knife you picked outa the wastebasket had a print that matched the hand on the door glass. A woman's left hand."

A long whistle slid through Marc's teeth. "So! You don't say. Why don't you tell me these things? How interesting!"

"Yeah, but what of it?"

"Haven't the slightest idea, Jerry. But I'll bet there's something to it."

"A woman. I don't get it."

He was interrupted by the jangle of his telephone.

"Yeah!—Yeah, speaking. . . . Good; where is he? . . . Well, bring him up. . . . Yeah, right away." He banged the receiver back on the hook. "One of the boys picked up the cab driver that taxied our girl friend away from the station last night. Now maybe we're getting somewhere. . . . Come in," he called as heavy steps sounded in the hall, followed by a knock on the door.

"You driving cab last night?" he asked of the chunky man twirling a cap nervously in his fingers.

"Yes sir."

"Pick up a woman wearing dark glasses at the station about midnight?"

"Yes sir."

"What did she look like? What was she wearing? Describe her."

"Well, she wasn't very tall, had on dark glasses, a dark brown cloth on her head, and a light tan coat. She had pretty legs," he added. "Awful pretty!"

"Suppose you were so busy looking at her legs you never saw her face," said Anderson sarcastically.

"Well, sir, I didn't see her very good," replied the driver. "It's kinda dark around the station."

"Where'd you take her?"

"Corner of Main and North."

"See where she went in?"

"I don't think she went in any place, sir. Leastwise not right there. She tells me to turn the corner off Main and stop in the middle of the block, and there ain't no building entrances there."

"Which way did she go?"

"I figgered it kinda funny, her getting out there, so I watches her. She started away from Main. That's all I know."

"Was there anyone else around?"

"Didn't see nobody on North. People around on Main Street, but that's a side street, and I don't think nobody was near."

"So you haven't any idea where she went?"

"No sir."

"Another dead end. Wonder where she was going. There's a hotel up that way, but we checked all the hotels. Okay, buddy. Leave your name at the desk. Might need you again."

"Possibly she lives here, and was coming home," Marc suggested.

"Yeah, but why'd she leave the cab in the middle of no place? And why'd she buy a ticket to Chicago and get off here?"

"Well, why'd Fat Face do the same thing?"

"Hey!" exclaimed Anderson. "D'you suppose those two were mixed up together?"

Marc shrugged. "Who knows? Only thing to do is find them and back-track."

"Yeah. Well, we'll have Fat Face when he comes for his bag—I hope. Come on; let's look at Richards' files."

"What did you find in Richards' clothes?" asked Marc as he and Anderson descended the steps of officialdom and climbed into a squad car.

"Oh, the usual stuff, nothing important. Keys, change, a watch, billfold with about four hundred bucks—not robbery anyway. A couple of letters, but no leads."

After a short ride through midday traffic the car pulled up at the entrance to the railroad office building. Taking an elevator to the sixth floor, Marc and Anderson entered the executive office.

The outer office was spacious, without being large. Deep red carpeting covered the floor completely. A desk angled across one corner under a big window, flanked on the right by a filing case, and on the left by a typewriter stand. A pair of chairs against the wall were the only other furnishings.

Miss Arthur sat at the desk staring out of the window. A clenched fist slowly polished a spot on the desk top. She turned toward the door as the two men entered. Her eyes were red disks in a chalky face. The fist stopped its polishing.

"Good morning, Miss Arthur," said Marc.

A mirthless smile twisted her lips. "Is it?" she snapped.

"No." Marc dropped his hat and coat on a chair and walked to the desk.

Anderson thrust his hands deep into his pockets and watched.

"Miss Arthur," continued Marc, throwing one leg over the corner of the desk, "we must look over Mr. Richards' files and correspondence. You have charge of them?"

She pushed hair back from her forehead and nodded wearily. "Yes, most of it. Mr. Richards—" Her voice cracked. She touched a handkerchief to her lips, coughed, and continued in a strained voice, almost a whisper, "Mr. Richards kept some things locked in his desk. Everything else is here, or in the case in his office." She pointed to a door marked "Private."

"Do you have a key to the desk?"

She shook her head.

"We'll break it open, then," said Marc, starting for the door. "Coming, Jerry?"

"Hold it a minute," growled Anderson. Plodding over to the desk, he leaned his paunch against the edge and glared at Miss Arthur. "Kinda overlooked you last night. How come you was on the car?"

She shrank from his eyes. Wrinkles creased furrows at the corners of her tight lips. She swayed slowly from side to side.

"Why, I went to Duck Lake at Mr. Richards' invitation. Is that strange?"

Anderson pursed his lips. "Mebbe not. Depends. A social visit?"

Miss Arthur hesitated. "Not entirely. I often went with Mr. Richards to take care of correspondence."

"Yeah? How long you been Richards' secretary?"

"About fifteen years."

"Quite a while. You're a good-looking gal. Ever play around with him? Sit on his lap? Spend a week-end in Florida?"

She gasped. A flush rose to her hair line and her clenched teeth showed through parted lips. Slowly she pushed herself to her feet, fury blazing from his bloodshot eyes.

"You beast!" she whispered. "You foul-minded swine!" Her hand flashed out and she slapped him, hard. Finger marks stood out clearly on his cheek.

Anderson stepped back in stunned surprise.

"Hey!" he roared. "You she-devil!"

He lunged across the desk and clutched her shoulder. She twisted away, backed into the corner and glared at him defiantly. He started around the desk, to be met by Marc, who was beside him with a bound.

"Jerry!" he said. "Cut it out!"

Anderson's breath whistled through distended nostrils. "Who does this wildcat think she is?"

"Mr. Richards' secretary. A lady. You'd better apologize."

"Apologize? To her?"

"Apologize."

"But darn it—"

"Jerry!" Marc shook him by the shoulder.

Slowly Anderson turned to the desk. Miss Arthur collapsed into her chair and her head dropped on her outstretched arms. Sobs shook her body.

"Okay," he mumbled. "I'm sorry, ma'am."

"That's better. This is where we go to work." Marc pushed Anderson toward the private office. Closing the door, he turned to him severely.

"You can't ride roughshod over a cultured woman like that, Jerry. She's no criminal."

"Yeah?" retorted Anderson. "She acted like one, resisting a officer. And she could've killed him!"

Marc nodded. "So she could. She's suspect, anyway, along with many others. Trouble is that now you've put her on guard."

"Nuts!"

"Did you bring Richards' keys?"

"Uh-huh. Figured we'd need 'em." Anderson pulled a key holder out of his pocket. "These presidents fix things nice," he said, admiring the spacious room with its soft carpet, huge walnut desk across one corner, and a profusion of leather chairs. Fumbling with a folder of keys, he found one that fitted the lock in the desk, and pulled out a large drawer. Several folders marked "Personal" were exposed. Piling them on top of the desk, he started sorting out the neatly filed papers. Marc pulled up a chair across the desk and reached for one of the folders.

"Might as well double up on this," he said, leafing through a similar stack. He scanned a confidential report from the superintendent of motive power on a new "eight hundred" type engine; a copy of a report from the traffic department on business from a new spur track; an estimate for a proposed signal extension; several other reports.

Closing the folder, Marc slid it toward Anderson and commenced on a second, a financial file with a check book showing a balance in five figures; a list of stocks and bonds; a slip of paper with a list of numbers. Marc copied the numbers into a notebook, and continued.

"I didn't know Richards was interested in old manuscripts," he exclaimed in surprise, studying the sheet in his hand.

"What you find?"

"Looks like a bill of sale. It's dated five years ago. 'Acknowledge receipt of $2,475.00 in full payment for original manuscript—Number 34,' and it's signed by Eric Linden! Clipped to it's another bill of sale, a copy, on a Lord Bookstore form, for the same manuscript and the same price, dated a week later. Looks like the sale just passed through Richards' hands." He handed the bills to Anderson.

"That's strange," said Anderson. "Wonder what Linden was doing with a paper that valuable."

"He's a collector. Mr. Barber says he's fanatical."

"Fanatical!" snorted Anderson. "Anyone who'll pay that kind of money for a pile of old paper is nuts! Where'd he get the dough, anyway?"

"Good question! Does seem a strange sale."

"Don't see's it does us much good. I'll ask Linden about it. Anything else?"

"Not yet."

"Oh boy!" exclaimed Anderson. He leaned back and chuckled, holding a piece of lavender note paper in his hand. "Listen to this! 'Darling Dicky: You are avoiding me! Why? Don't you ever think of our beautiful times together? Moonlight and nightingales. I can't bear to have you so near and yet so far—' and so on. It's signed—'I love you, Dorene.' Wow! The old son-of-a-gun."

"Give me that!" cried Marc, snatching the letter from Anderson's hand. He read it, and handed it back.

"Fools there are," he said. "The woman should never have written that, and Richards should never have kept it."

"Who's 'Dorene,' I wonder?"

Marc tugged at the lobe of his ear reflectively. "It might be—just might possibly be—Mrs. Dorene Johnson. Are there any more like it?"

"Yeah. Couple more. The last one's dated six months ago. . . . Johnson!" The explosive ejaculation brought Anderson up rigid. "Did you say Johnson? The wife of one of our suspects?"

Marc nodded. "Pure conjecture, but the name's rather unusual. It shouldn't be too hard to check."

"Well, well," chuckled Anderson. "We progress. By gosh, we progress. This's something good to work on."

"Not so fast, Jerry," cautioned Marc. "You still have no proof against Johnson. It may not be Mrs. Johnson, and if it is, he may not know about the affair. It's a possibility only."

"Don't I know it?" snapped Anderson. "You don't have to tell me my business. But it's the first thing that makes sense. Banker Johnson'll bear a little investigation. I'll just keep these souvenirs."

Marc smiled ironically. "A nice juicy love triangle always makes sense, doesn't it, Jerry?"

Both men continued their search in silence for several minutes. Marc selected a letter on thin carbon copy paper, and wrinkled his brow in perplexity.

"This's strange," he said. "Here's a copy of a letter to Abercrombie and Coyle, Auditors, in Chicago. It's signed by D. Arnold, and explains a delay in the current audit of the books of the railroad. It says that there's an apparent shortage of some fifteen hundred dollars, and states that a re-audit is being made. What do you make of that?" Marc handed the letter to Anderson.

Glancing at it, Anderson returned it in disgust. "Don't bother me with your troubles, Jordan. Not my fault if you fellows can't keep your business straight."

Marc pondered over a longhand written note at the bottom of the page, "Checked H. A.—10/2/36—A." He rose and slowly walked to the outer office. Miss Arthur had controlled her weeping, and sat as she had when first they entered. Ignoring a wadded handkerchief on the desk, Marc laid down the letter.

"Sorry to bother you, Miss Arthur," he said crisply, "but this letter—did you add the note?"

She glanced at it, and shook her head.

"No," she said softly. "It was probably Mrs. Ashley, Mr. Gordon's secretary."

"Where can I find her?"

"Directly across the hall."

Marc followed directions to an office duplicating Richards' and asked the same question of the young woman working busily at a typewriter.

"Yes, Mr. Jordan," she said. "Miss Arthur was out and I took that call."

"I see," said Marc. A shadow of disappointment flashed across his face. "Thank you, Mrs. Ashley."

Returning to Richards' office, he added the letter to the pile on the desk, and for some time the search continued.

Finishing a folder, Marc stretched lazily and lit a cigarette.

"Well, Jerry, I've work to do. Can't help you much here. Miss Arthur might help you, if you are nice to her!"

Anderson glanced up absently. "Sure—sure. Looks like this's a waste of time, but it's got to be done."

"Good luck. I'll see you later."

Closing the door to Richards' office, Marc strode rapidly across the corridor to a door marked "Mr. Linden."

"Good morning, Miss Jones. Mr. Linden in?"

"No, Mr. Jordan. He hasn't come in this morning."

"Any word from him?"

"No, sir. Of course, he was expecting to be in Chicago today, but I suppose his plans have been changed."

"Yes," said Marc dryly, "they've been changed. He lives on Westchester, is that right?"

"Apartment 3D, 1410 Westchester."

"Thank you. If Linden comes in, will you tell him that I'd like to see him, please?"

The girl nodded and Marc left the office. He rode the elevator to the street level and walked thoughtfully out of the building.

7

Walking slowly down Main Street, with his hat on the back of his head, Marc turned into a side street and studied the signs on a heterogeneous collection of stores.

He finally stopped in front of Lord's Bookstore, and looked at the display in the window. One side was stuffed with second-hand books of all kinds. In the center of the other window a tattered copy of "Dead Eye Dick" had the place of honor in a glass frame. Surrounding it were several copies of old dime novels—relics of the days when women wore bustles, and men wore guns. Stepping into the dim interior, reeking with the mustiness and dust of ancient paper, he was greeted by a small, stoop-shouldered man.

"Good morning, sir. What can I do for you?"

"Good morning," replied Marc. "Are you Mr. Lord?"

"That's right, young man."

"You've an interesting place, Mr. Lord." Marc glanced around at the stacks of books "I imagine you have some rare copies tucked away on your shelves."

"Oh, most of this stuff is trash," replied Lord, waving his hand in disdain. "It's revolting the things people read these days. Are you a book lover, sir?"

"Well—" Marc hesitated. "In a way, yes. Do you have anything on criminal law?"

"Yes, indeed, a very fine selection. Just step this way, please." Lord led the way to the back of the store. "There are editions you won't find anywhere else in this part of the country." He pointed to a shelf proudly.

"I believe an acquaintance of mine is one of your customers," said Marc casually, thumbing through one of the books. "Mr. Eric Linden."

"Oh, yes, Mr. Linden," exclaimed Lord, his eyes lighting with pleasure. "He's a true book lover. Mr. Linden's been a good customer of mine for many years—one of the best. I've been fortunate enough to obtain many rare items for him in years past. If you're a friend of his, that's an excellent recommendation." He smiled warmly at Marc.

"Oh, I'm not exactly a friend," replied Marc apologetically, "just an acquaintance. You say he's been purchasing books from you for some time?"

"Many years. Mr. Linden's a collector, a true connoisseur. I'm proud to say that he patronizes me almost exclusively. He frequently visits dealers in other cities, but arranges purchases through me."

"Some of these books are quite expensive, aren't they?"

"A few are almost priceless. The value depends upon the number of known copies in existence. Sometimes a copy which originally sold for ten cents will be worth several hundred, or even several thousand dollars."

"You don't have such copies on display, do you?"

"Indeed not. That'd be foolish," replied Lord. "In fact, I keep very few valuable books on hand. Customers for such items are scarce, and I can't afford the investment."

"Then how are sales arranged?"

"Usually by specific request for a certain edition, or by a general understanding such as I have with Mr. Linden. I call all good items to his attention as I find them. Only a few months ago I arranged for the purchase of a first edition 'Pickwick' for him. You'd be surprised, young man, to know what that volume cost."

"What did it cost?" asked Marc, watching Lord intently out of the corner of his eye.

"Such information is confidential," replied Lord. "Perhaps Mr. Linden would tell you, if you asked him. Collectors are sometimes jealous and secretive about such matters."

"I understand. Tell me, Mr. Lord, have you ever had any dealings with Mr. Richards?"

"You mean Mr. Richards, the man who was murdered last night? Terrible thing, isn't it? Yes, I did once handle a transaction for Mr. Richards several years ago. I recall the occasion because it was very puzzling to me."

"In what way?"

"Mr. Richards came to me with a manuscript—a very valuable item—and asked me to sell it for him. I was immediately suspicious, because I had obtained that manuscript for Mr. Linden some time before through a very fortunate transaction, and I knew he valued it highly. I didn't know Mr. Richards, and naturally first supposed that he had come by it illegally. Mr. Linden agreed, however, that everything was in order, so of course I was glad to handle the matter for Mr. Richards."

"I don't see anything strange about that," said Marc. "Just a straightforward sale."

"I forgot the peculiar part," continued Lord. "Mr. Richards specified a price—I've forgotten what, exactly—but some odd figure, and insisted that it should be sold for that, no more and no less. I tried to tell him that the manuscript was worth more, but he was adamant. He told me to sell it for anything I liked, so long as he got that particular amount of money. Naturally, I made a nice profit. Perhaps that's why I remember the sale."

"Did Linden say why he sold it to Richards?"

"I didn't see Mr. Linden for quite some time after that. It was nearly a year before he made any more purchases. I did ask him about it, but he refused to discuss the matter. He said the deal was closed, and he wanted to forget about it. I think he regretted the sale."

"I suppose Linden had good reasons for selling. How much are you asking for this book?" Marc indicated the volume he was idly fingering.

"That book," said Lord, examining an incomprehensible hieroglyphic on the inside cover, "is ten dollars, and a real bargain at the price. There are only a few hundred of these in existence."

"I'm sure it's a bargain," said Marc dryly, fishing for his wallet. "I believe I'll take it. Will you hold it, please, and I'll stop in the first opportunity?"

"Be glad to, sir. What name shall I put on it?"

"Marc Jordan. It may be several days before I get back."

"All right, Mr. Jordan. We'll be glad to see you any time."

Marc walked slowly out of the store, his forehead furrowed by a thoughtful frown. Turning into Main Street again, he hailed a passing cab, and gave an address on Riverside Drive.

His brow was still furrowed when the cab turned into a white gravel drive and stopped at the entrance to a beautiful colonial house overlooking a wide sweep of lawn, and a bend of the river. Instructing the driver to wait, Marc climbed the steps to the veranda and pressed the bell. In a few minutes the door was opened a crack by a trim maid in white cap and apron. Tear-stained eyes met his questioningly.

"Is Mrs. Arnold at home?" asked Marc.

"Yes, sir, she's home," replied the maid, "but she won't

see anyone."

"It's important that I do see her," said Marc, drawing out a card and hastily scribbling a note. "Please take this to her, and tell her that I'll only need to take up a few minutes of her time."

"Yes, sir," answered the maid, taking the card and disappearing into the house.

Marc paced back and forth across the veranda impatiently. Shortly the door opened and the maid motioned for him to enter.

"Mrs. Arnold will see you, sir," she said. "Step into the library, please. She'll be right down."

Marc glanced around at his surroundings. He had always liked this house. Richards had built it soon after his marriage. It was beautifully arranged and furnished, but not in the grand manner. Richards had been a long way from the president of a railroad then. A large window in the end of the library looked out over the river. Marc was standing before this window admiring the beauty of the scene when his thoughts were interrupted by a light step.

"Good morning, Marc."

He turned to find Joan standing in the doorway, dressed from chin to toe in a tailored housecoat. Her pale face, though grief-stricken, was composed, and he was relieved to see that in spite of the dark circles under her eyes, they had regained some of their natural sparkle.

"Good morning, Miss Joan," he said quietly. "My apologies for disturbing you. It's good of you to see me."

"I'm all right now, Marc," she replied, her voice trembling a little. "It's been a terrible shock to me, I can't quite realize how terrible yet. But Daddy's gone, and all I want is to have the criminal caught."

Marc smiled at her in admiration. "Miss Joan, you're brave. Your father'd be proud of you."

"If I can help, I'll be glad."

"I think you can. Could you bear to have me run through the events of yesterday as we know them?"

"Yes, I guess so," said Joan, biting her lip. "Go ahead."

"Correct me if you don't agree, or if I make any mistakes. All of you were at Duck Lake except Linden, who was in St. Paul. You drove from the lake to your father's private car in your station wagon and got on the car sometime after seven o'clock. The Chicago Flyer picked up the car at seven-thirty, and Linden joined you. Correct so far?"

At Joan's nod, Marc continued.

"Your father, Miss Arthur, Linden, Johnson, and presumably your husband were going to Chicago to a convention."

"Not Dave," interrupted Joan. "His home office is in Chicago, you know. He works for Abercrombie and Coyle, though he's here most of the time. He's busy on the annual audit and was going back to attend to some work there. I was just going along for the ride."

"I see," continued Marc. "Anyway, you all got together and had dinner on the train. That was the arrangement. After dinner the men played bridge; you and Miss Arthur went to bed at nine-thirty. By the way, did you go directly to sleep?"

"No, I read until Dave came in."

"Did Miss Arthur leave the men at exactly the same time that you did?"

Joan thought a minute. "Yes, we went out together."

"How'd she get along with your father?"

"Poor Miss Arthur! She adored Dad. She wore her heart on her sleeve, and he never noticed."

"Umm. The bridge game broke up about ten-thirty. Your father and Linden went to their rooms. Did you hear anything at that time?"

"No. The car's so heavy, it's quite soundproof."

"Then your husband came to bed, at what time?"

"A little after eleven. Six or seven minutes after."

"You remember, I said that it might be important. It is. Johnson said that your husband left the lounge at eleven-seven. Since the murder weapon—the axe—was found at Zola Crossing, and since the train passed the crossing at ten fifty-eight according to O'Conner's automatic chart, the crime must have been committed before Dave left the lounge.

"Johnson was the last to go to bed. He was alone in the lounge for some time, and there's no verification of when he left. Is that a correct statement of the timetable?"

"As far as I know, yes."

"Tell me, Miss Joan—how shall I put it?— what was the atmosphere of your gathering? How did the various members act, particularly your father? Was there any obvious strain?"

Joan shook her head. "No. Daddy seemed perfectly natural." She suppressed a catch in her voice and continued. "He was always blunt, and a little intolerant. The relations in that group are tense, but I don't think it was any worse than usual."

"Tense? In what way?"

"Daddy and Dave sometimes rubbed each other the wrong way. They're so much alike—both fighters. Daddy seemed to enjoy bullying people, particularly Mr. Linden. Mr. Linden's such a quiet, mousy little man. I think Daddy was especially mean to him."

"How about Mr. Johnson?"

"Oh, they got along all right."

"Tell me about Mrs. Johnson. She's quite young, isn't she?"

Joan studied Marc intently, her eyes veiled with suspicion. "Why do you ask about her?"

Marc shrugged. "No particular reason, except that the family of anyone involved is of interest."

"She's a cat!" said Joan bitterly, then added hastily, "No, that isn't fair. But I don't like her. You know, Marc, sometimes a man can sense when another man is crooked. A woman can sense the same thing in another woman, and that's the way I feel about her."

"How long have they been married?"

"About six years. They were married a year before Dave and I. They bought the summer home next to ours, and the very first summer she started making eyes at Daddy! She doesn't love her husband!"

"Why do you say that?"

"Any woman who doesn't show a little affection in public doesn't show much in private. She treats Mr. Johnson like dirt. She's much nicer to all other men—even Dave!"

"Oh!" said Marc. "The green god. What does Dave say?"

"Laughs it off. He's used to pretty women who sigh over him. What am I saying? I must be upset, to talk this way."

"D'you think Mr. Johnson suspected there was any friendliness between his wife and your father?" Marc watched her closely.

"I don't know. He's a silent fish. Comes of being a banker, I guess. When Daddy got mad he'd blast everyone around, but I've never seen Mr. Johnson anything but calm."

"Mr. Barber told me he was making a new will. Did you know that?"

"Yes. Daddy talked it over with us. Both he and Dave thought it made better provision for me. Dave was glad to avoid the responsibility."

"Is your husband in?" asked Marc, offering a cigarette to Joan.

"No," she replied, inhaling deeply. "Dave went out about an hour ago. He had some business to attend to."

"I've bothered you enough. Anything else you can think of?"

"I'm afraid not, Marc."

"If you have any hunches, let me know. I'm working with the police."

"I will, Marc. You were on the car last night before the police; did you see Cleo?"

"Cleo?" exclaimed Marc in surprise. "I don't understand."

"Cleopatra, my poodle. She was around all evening, but in the excitement naturally I forgot about her. I'm afraid she wandered away."

"No," replied Marc. "I didn't see a dog."

"She's such a friendly little thing. I hope she didn't fall off the platform. Would you speak to the men about her? Someone might find her."

"Sure. One thing more—did your father have a safe?"

"Yes, in his den. Why?"

"I'd like to look through it. Do you have the combination?"

"No. No one but he had it."

"Hm," murmured Marc. "Perhaps I do. Where's the safe? May I see it?"

Joan led the way to a small room on the second floor. A large window overlooked the river; the panorama was even more impressive because of the added height. A large leather chair was placed before the window. The room was tastefully furnished with other comfortable chairs, a small writing desk, and a fireplace in one end. Built into the wall beside the fireplace was a small safe.

Marc referred to the list of numbers he had copied from Richards' file, twiddled the dial, and finally swung the door open. His eyes glittered with curiosity as he surveyed the row of drawers. The first contained a large sum of money. The second, stocks and bonds; a number of mortgages. The third, an odd assortment of jewelry: a pearl necklace; a wedding ring; a gold locket. In the fourth drawer, a large manila envelope held the solitary place of honor. The envelope contained a report dated Sept. 1, 19—.

To: J. C. Richards
From: Jonathan Thatcher
Subject: Mrs. Dorene Johnson
This report summarizes to date, on assignment, re above subject.

Dorene Johnson—nee Jane Doenette—alias Kitty Dean—alias Dorene Dean. Born 19— in Cicero, Illinois, to Angelo and Jane Doenette. Grade school. High school, one year. Father disappeared soon after Jane's birth. Present whereabouts unknown. Mother died when Jane was sixteen.

Worked South State Street restaurant two years as waitress. Resided South Side, two years—no visible means of support. Committed reform school—eighteen months.

Assumed name Kitty Dean. Danced Rialto Burlesque—three years. Seen frequently with one David Arnold.

Vaudeville stage in knife-throwing act—ten months.

Minor dancing part in musical show. Assumed name Dorene Dean. Approached by one Arthur Johnson. Married same in two months. At present living as Mrs. Arthur Johnson, Calumet.
Signed:
J. Thatcher
Thatcher Detective Agency

Marc slowly folded the report and tucked it into the envelope. Glancing compassionately at the girl sitting in her father's chair and staring out of the window, he slipped the envelope into his pocket and closed the safe.

"Seems to be mostly cash and valuables," he said. "I thought there might be something more important. I'll leave you the combination, Miss Joan. You'll want to go through the safe yourself." He tore the sheet with the numbers from his notebook and handed it to her.

"Thank you, Marc. That'll save me trouble. Did you find what you were looking for?"

"I didn't know what to look for," he said evasively. "You've helped me, though. Hope it hasn't tired you."

"No, talking has relieved me. Perhaps I'll be able to get some rest now. Can you let yourself out?"

"Of course. Please don't worry, Miss Joan. This'll be cleared up soon. I'd like to visit Duck Lake. Is there anyone there now?"

"Yes, Mrs. Donovan, our housekeeper, lives there all the time. She's difficult, but if you tell her I sent you, it'll be all right."

"Thank you." Marc's mouth twitched with sympathy as the slim girl left him. The world is full of all kinds of people, he thought bitterly; all kinds.

Running down the steps to the waiting cab, he gave the driver an address, and pulled savagely on a cigarette.

8

Arriving at the Union Office Building, Marc paid the driver and stood on the curb staring at a wad of tobacco resting in a puddle of water in the gutter. Did he imagine it, or did the tobacco really resemble the sweep of a woman's carefully tended pompadour? Turning away in disgust, he strode into the building, consulted the directory posted beside the elevator, and rode to the eleventh floor.

He walked slowly down the corridor, examining names on the doors. At an angle in the corridor he was jarred roughly by a man hurrying in the opposite direction.

"Why the devil don't you look where you're going?" snapped an angry voice.

"Pardon me, Arnold," replied Marc calmly, "but why don't you look where *you're* going?"

"Oh, hello, Jordan. Didn't recognize you." Arnold stared at Marc.

"Where are you going?"

"Aren't you being overly personal?"

"Possibly." Marc straightened his coat and brushed a speck of dust from his sleeve. "Under the circumstances, I was surprised to find your charming wife alone, when I called this morning."

"What're you up to, Jordan?" demanded Arnold. "Why can't you leave her alone? Stop sticking your nose into other people's affairs, understand?"

"Why, Dave," replied Marc lightly, "one would be led to believe you're upset. What are you afraid of?"

"Nothing," replied Arnold. "I'm sorry, Jordan. This business has me on edge. Things have happened so fast the last few days that I'm not myself."

"The last few days—yes," murmured Marc. "Well, you'd better get yourself in hand, my friend. The police'll be around to ask questions. You might give a bad impression. Inspector Anderson's feelings are easily hurt."

"I see what you mean. Accept my apologies, will you, and forget it." He extended his hand to Marc.

"All right, Arnold," replied Marc. "Only remember your wife's taking this bravely. Take good care of her. She'd be hard to replace."

He watched Arnold disappear into the elevator with puzzled wonder, and continued his search. Opening a door marked: "Thatcher Detective Agency," he was met by the cold stare of a burly individual who appeared to combine the functions of doorman and bouncer.

"Mr. Thatcher in?" he asked.

"Yeah. Who wants to know?"

Marc selected one of his cards and handed it to the man in silence. He disappeared through an inner door, to reappear a minute later.

"In here," he said sullenly.

Marc walked into the inner office and considered the man seated behind a chipped oak desk. He was big. Dark brown hair, streaked with gray, was slicked straight back. He sat with both hands on the top of the desk, palms down, and returned Marc's stare with the vivacity of a brick wall.

"Jordan?" he asked in a flat voice.

"That's correct," replied Marc. "Mr. Thatcher?"

"Yeah. Come in and sit down. What's on your mind?"

"Quite a number of things, Thatcher, but most of them'd bore you." Marc lit a cigarette and gulped a mouthful of smoke. "I wonder, for instance, if you're a gambler?"

"What d'you mean?" Thatcher's eyes narrowed with suspicion.

"I wonder if you'd care to place a bet of—say ten dollars—that I can't name your last client?"

"Quit stalling, Jordan," snapped Thatcher. "What're you getting at?"

"Will you take the bet?"

"I wouldn't bet with one of you shysters that black was black if I saw it! Now, what're you up to?"

"I discovered by accident—an almost fatal accident—that your last caller was Dave Arnold. Right?"

"What of it?"

"Thanks, Thatcher! Mind telling me what Arnold wanted?"

"You bet I mind! None of your damn business. That all you wanted to know?"

"By no means, Mr. Thatcher. That was just an accident. I want to discuss this interesting document which came into my possession—also by accident. Do you recognize it?" he asked, taking the report from his pocket and holding it for Thatcher to see.

Thatcher, making no move to take the report, glanced at it, and returned his stare to Marc. "Yeah, I recognize it. What're you doing with it?"

"Good question." Marc tilted his chair against the wall and examined the paper. "Very good indeed. Of course you've read the morning papers."

"Of course I've read the morning papers!" snapped Thatcher. "Now come out with it, Jordan. My time is valuable."

"All right, Thatcher." Marc banged the legs of his chair against the floor and leaned across the desk. "You know that J. C. Richards, president of the C. M. Railroad, was murdered on his own private car last night—practically chopped in two with an axe. I'm interested in the investigation of his murder. You know Anderson. He's a mighty fine traffic cop, and passable at the County Fair, but he'll never find this murderer. I ran onto this scrap of paper in the course of the investigation, and under the circumstances it seemed rather important. Your name is appended, so I came straight to you. Come now, Thatcher—give!"

"You have the report; why bother me?"

"Oh, but I've a feeling—intuition perhaps—that there's much more than appears on the surface of this sheet of paper. For instance, how did it happen that Richards came to you in the first place, and why did he want this information?"

"I haven't the slightest idea."

"You know, Thatcher," said Marc, coolly blowing a smoke ring toward the ceiling, and surveying the room, "you've a nice place here. Spacious office, good protection—that sliding iron door didn't grow there, did it?—indicate an extensive clientele. I imagine your office rent is—well, not inconsiderable. It's strange that we never hear about you. I don't recall seeing your name in the public press for some time. Mere chance, I presume, or could it be deliberate? Is it due to a desire for privacy? Could you yearn to stay in the wings in preference to being the leading man up by the footlights?"

"Keep talking."

"Meditating's the word. And meditating along such lines, the inevitable conclusion is that you shun publicity."

"Yes?"

"Yes. That's unfortunate." Marc carefully knocked the ash from the end of his cigarette. "Because I feel sure that Inspector Anderson'll insist upon considerable publicity when this interesting document becomes part of his glossary of information. His lack of intellect notwithstanding, Inspector Anderson's a very thorough man and inclined to turn over all stones. In this case I'd expect arduous stone work!"

"Are you trying to say, Jordan," asked Thatcher, his blunt fingers beating a rhythm on the desk top, "that if I let you pump me, you'll suppress the report?"

"Heaven forbid, Mr. Thatcher! I'd suggest no such thing. If this report proves vital, the police'll have to have it. However, I'm not at all sure that it is vital, except to point the way to further investigation. At some later date the report—mislaid perhaps, or overlooked—will turn up. I don't believe you'll find it hard to imagine the catcalls the gentlemen of the press'll raise if Anderson gets his hands on this morsel. The name 'Thatcher' might figure prominently in some of the catcalls."

"Hang it, Jordan, I don't mess with criminal cases. They're poison. I don't intend to start now."

"Pardon me." Marc tapped a lean finger on the desk. "You're in a criminal case now—in up to your neck. I'm giving you one chance to ease out and keep the Thatcher name unbesmirched, on the chance that you know something that may help clear this thing up."

"Will you guarantee to keep us out of it?"

"I'll guarantee nothing, except that if you don't give me straight answers to a few questions, I'll be forced—forced, mind you—to turn this report over to Anderson—at once."

Thatcher heaved a deep sigh and dropped his hands in a gesture of surrender. "All right, Jordan. What do you want?"

Marc tipped his chair back against the wall and hooked his feet under the rungs. "My respect for the Thatcher Detective Agency has mounted tremendously," he said dryly. "Is your report complete?"

"Complete? I don't get you."

"I mean, does it contain all the information you've been able to collect?"

Thatcher considered Marc thoughtfully for a moment and then said slowly, "No, it doesn't."

"A dentist pulling teeth has a snap compared to me pulling information out of you. What's left out?"

Again Thatcher hesitated. "Kitty Dean left the show for six months. Nervous breakdown, she told them."

A long whistle escaped Marc's lips. "Not—?"

"Can't prove it. We weren't able to trace her, but there were indications."

"Arnold?"

Thatcher shook his head. "Don't think so. However, he had a marriage license at one time."

"But it doesn't make sense. Why didn't they get married instead of all the hush-hush?"

"Miss Dean said she wouldn't marry anyone but a millionaire. Quite vocal about it. Seems the millionaire turned up."

"A gold digger of the old school," murmured Marc. "Any idea how Arnold took it?"

"Not too seriously. He dropped out, and started with the accounting firm."

"How did he happen to go with Abercrombie and Coyle?"

"Arnold's smart as a whip, as you know. He's very capable, and sold himself to Abercrombie."

"How'd it happen that Miss Dean dropped out of vaudeville, and started dancing on her own?"

Thatcher chuckled. "She didn't drop out; she was knocked out! Her knife-throwing partner took one too many one night, and pinned her to the wall. A knife went through her right arm just above the elbow. Her arm was practically useless for months."

Marc toyed idly with his watch chain. "How'd Richards react to all this?"

"He was pleased with the dope on Mrs. Johnson, but quite upset when he learned about Arnold."

Marc smiled. "I can guess how he felt. Now answer my first question. Why did Richards come to you in the first place?"

"He'd never say, but I think we can both guess."

"How long've you worked on the case?"

"Six months or so. About two months ago we got our first real information."

"Did you tell Richards everything you've told me?"

"Of course."

"The report—did he request it in this form?"

"Yes. He said something about wanting a club."

Marc rose slowly and paced the length of the office. Stopping before a window overlooking the city, he gazed out unseeingly. After several minutes of silence he dropped back into his chair.

"What did Arnold want with you this morning? He was certainly on the jump when I saw him."

"He tried to pump me." Thatcher laughed mirthlessly. "I feel like a well this morning."

"The price you pay for prying into other people's business," said Marc, grinning at him. "Did you let yourself be pumped?"

"Not much!"

"What did he think you knew?"

"I don't know. He wanted to know if I'd been working for Richards, and why. He used the same argument that you did, that he's working on a solution of Richards' murder. He said he had an idea who did it, and was looking for proof. However, with nothing but his word to go on, I didn't tell him a thing."

"He's probably worried—with reason—about how Joan will take his—ah, colorful past! She loves him, but probably couldn't stomach all this at once. Did he say how he happened to come to you?"

"No."

For some time both men silently considered the whims of mankind. Then Marc asked, "This report—did it conclude your assignment?"

Thatcher frowned thoughtfully. "No, it didn't. I've had a tail on Mrs. Johnson for weeks."

Marc leaned across the desk, his eyes glittering with excited interest.

"No! Wonderful!" he breathed. "How about last night? Were you shadowing her yesterday?"

"Yes. My man's back. I called him in this morning. In view of events, that job's probably wound up. No use running up expenses," he said dryly.

"Is he here now? Could I talk to him?"

Thatcher considered. "Well, I've gone this far with you, Jordan. No use holding out now."

He pressed a bell button under his desk and the blank-eyed guard thrust his head through the door.

"See if Mike's around. Send him in," ordered Thatcher.

Marc paced a crack in the floor nervously, hands thrust deep into his pockets. After a brief wait, a florid, thick-set man entered.

"Want me, Boss?"

"Uh-huh," grunted Thatcher. "Jordan, Mike Klutz, one of my operators. Jordan wants to ask you about yesterday. Tell him anything he wants to know."

Klutz eyed Marc with suspicion. "Cop?"

Marc shook his head. "No. Just dabbling in a private investigation. I understand you've been having a vacation at Duck Lake?"

Klutz scowled with disgust. "Vacation? Are you kiddin'? Tailin' is tailin', Duck Lake or wherever. A helluva way to earn a livin'!"

"But you've been at Duck Lake on a job, that right?"

Glancing questioningly at Thatcher, Klutz nodded. "Yeah, that's right."

"And you were checking up on a very attractive lady, Mrs. Arthur Johnson?"

"Yeah."

"Tell me," continued Marc, "what were Mrs. Johnson's activities yesterday?"

"She didn't have none, except to stay home."

Marc's jaw sagged in surprise. "You mean she was at home all day? She didn't go out?"

"That's right: she was and she didn't."

"You're sure of that?"

"Sure. I was parked up the road a piece where I could watch the house. It sets right on the lake. No way to leave by that side."

"Except by boat," said Marc dryly.

"Well," replied Klutz reluctantly, "that's right, but she didn't. I seen her around the yard off and on all day."

"How long were you there?"

"I left around eight-thirty. It's dark then. Mr. Johnson had left with the bunch next door. The lights went off downstairs, so I figured she'd gone to bed, and left."

"So you don't know what happened after eight-thirty?"

"That's right. Them's my orders," he said defensively. "Soon's they close up for the night, I leave. A man can't hang around twenty-four hours a day."

Marc resumed his pacing around the office, disappointment written on his face. "No, I guess you're right. Yesterday was a dull and peaceful day. How about this morning?"

"I called him at the hotel before he left," interrupted Thatcher. "He came in from there, didn't you?"

"That's right, Boss," replied Klutz.

Marc shook his head sadly. "I was hoping we had something."

"That all you wanted, Jordan?" asked Thatcher. "Okay, Mike, beat it," he said as Marc nodded assent. Klutz disappeared through the door and Thatcher resumed his finger-tapping exercise.

"This man Klutz, is he good?"

"All my men're good."

"Did he ever report a meeting between Mrs. Johnson and David Arnold?"

Thatcher considered. "Yes, about a week ago Mrs. Johnson went out in her car in the middle of the afternoon. She drove around the lake to a picnic place in the woods. Klutz followed. Arnold came along in a speed boat and picked her up. They were gone about an hour. Of course all Klutz could do was sit and wait. After a while she came back, got into her car and went home."

"How'd she act when she got back?"

"She almost ran into Klutz coming out, and never saw him."

"Has he reported her meeting anyone else?"

"No."

"Did he ever lose her for any length of time?"

"Once. His car quit on him one day when she drove out."

Marc threw a knee over the corner of the desk. "You've given me a lot of information, Thatcher. How much're you holding out?"

Thatcher returned Marc's stare blandly. "I've answered all your questions."

"So you have," replied Marc grimly. "Now may I recommend a course of action: namely, that we keep our little tête-à-tête between ourselves? It'd be highly undesirable to muddy the stream any more than necessary. There are expert mud-stirrers about."

Thatcher grunted. "You're wasting breath telling me that!"

"I'm sure of it." Marc walked to the door and turned with a wave of his hat. "Thanks, Thatcher. You'll be hearing from me again."

Hurrying through the outer office, he weathered the stare of the door tender, and reached the corridor. Thatcher must be expecting trouble, to keep a husky like that at the door, he thought.

Straddling a stool at a lunch counter, Marc ordered a sandwich and coffee and was deeply engrossed scribbling notes in a notebook when his train of thought was interrupted by a soft voice from the next seat.

"Don't look now, but that waitress, the one with the figure, is going to stick a butcher knife in the short order cook any minute!"

Marc turned to meet Nora's teasing eyes.

"How's it going, Sherlock?" she asked.

"Hello, Irish," grinned Marc. "Thought you might get hungry about this time. Of course, mooching a free lunch has nothing whatever to do with the happy coincidence of your arrival! Just my magnetic personality, no doubt."

"Okay, stingy, I'll buy my own lunch. In fact, I'll buy yours too."

"Nora, darling, this's so sudden!"

"Oh, stop it. How is the great investigation?"

"Progress no end. Hunks of it. So much that I'm considering taking the afternoon off for a vacation."

"Marc, you're fooling. I know it."

"No, really," replied Marc lightly. "Think I'll take a trip to Duck Lake this afternoon. I understand fishing's fine there this fall and thought I'd check up on it. How about coming along for the ride?"

"Mr. Jordan, have you forgotten, I'm a woiking goil."

Marc leaned over and whispered confidentially in her ear. "We'll tell Beak Nose I'm going on important business and simply *must* have secretarial assistance."

"It's a beautiful day," said Nora, gazing wistfully at the sunlight streaming across the counter. "Maybe it could be fixed. No one's doing a bit of work anyway, and Beak Nose is running around in a fuddle."

"That's settled then. I'll fire up the Ford and meet you at the office. One-thirty. It's about a three-hour drive, if we hurry."

"What're you really going for, Marc? You have that long nose into something, I'll bet."

"I'm just playing a hunch," said Marc. "I don't know what I'm going for. This thing's a muddle. The pieces don't fit. For example, where'd Cleo get to?"

"Cleo?" exclaimed Nora in astonishment. "That's a new name!"

"Yes. Joan Arnold's pet poodle. It got away last night."

"Why, he probably wandered off when no one was looking. Dogs have been known to do that, you know."

"She! The name's Cleopatra. And if she wandered off, someone should soon find her. Hope so. It might help."

"I can't see what a dog has to do with it."

"Neither can I. That's what worries me. Let's eat. Time flies and we have things to do."

9

The gray Ford nosed its way through traffic with the instinct of a hound trailing a rabbit. As the outskirts of the city were reached, it settled down to a smooth, purring run over the open highway. The wind, puffing through the open window, whipped Nora's hair into whirlwind swirls and stung her cheeks a rosy pink, to the shame of man-made color. Marc glanced at her appreciatively.

"Fun, isn't it?"

"Gorgeous! Though the way you drive does give a girl the shivers. Why I risk my future, with all its beautiful possibilities, in your callous hands, I don't know."

"May I be permitted to guess?"

"Never mind! Isn't the country simply beautiful? Look at those hills." She pointed to the hillside splashed with a riot of red, orange and yellow.

"The Great Painter gone berserk. Frustrated and repressed the summer through, He bursts the bonds, casts aside His brush of green and lays about with exotic color."

"Why, Marc! You amaze me. A poet!" Nora turned teasing eyes on him.

"Oh, not at all. I've many talents," said Marc modestly. "You should investigate them. I'm handsome, intelligent, ambitious; everyone likes me. In short, I fail to see how you can resist my charm!"

Nora gazed at the paint pot woods. "I sometimes wonder about that myself," she murmured.

Marc shed his mockery like a zippered coat. His hand pressed her cool palm lying on the seat beside him. "Do I detect a certain warmth of feeling?" he asked softly.

Nora's eyes met his. "I don't know, Marc." Disengaging her hand, she tucked a loose strand of hair under her scarf. "Shall we postpone this? We've important business to consider."

Marc sighed reluctantly. "Unfortunately, that's only too true. These surroundings had momentarily banished all the problems of life. What a mess! I'm afraid things are going to get thick before we're through."

"Is Inspector Anderson making progress?"

"Inspector Anderson is unquestionably making progress, but I doubt that it'll result in an arrest," said Marc. "Perhaps it's unfair to berate the law, but Anderson is singularly lacking in imagination. Unless I'm very wrong, this is a highly imaginative murder."

Nora shuddered. "It doesn't seem imaginative to me, just brutal and sordid. Someone hated Mr. Richards and killed him with an axe. The axe came from their car, so it must have been someone in that car. Find who had reason to kill him, and that's the murderer."

"Wish it were as simple as that," replied Marc grimly. "But you don't have all the facts. Neither do I, not by a long way. It's sordid and brutal, but so were the lives of some of the principals. I'm beginning to suspect that we'll find half a dozen people with plenty of motive for murder. And the fact that the axe was taken from Richards' car doesn't prove a thing. Far as we know, no one saw it taken. There was plenty of time for anyone to take it, including all the people in the rest of the train."

"I'd forgotten that," said Nora. "It could've been anyone on the train, and that's a lot of people. Have you located any of them?"

"A few. Only two look suspicious, a man and a woman —not together as far as we know. Neither has been located. There are other puzzling things. We found a wicked-looking knife—it could be a fine kitchen knife—under the drinking fountain. Nothing particularly suspicious about it—no bloodstains for instance—except that it was there, less than fifteen feet from Mr. Richards."

"Aren't you being melodramatic?"

Marc shook his head. "Possibly, but that's not all. What was a bloody towel doing under Johnson's berth? I had to talk fast to keep Anderson from arresting Johnson on the spot. That might have been a serious mistake. And what about the water stains on the back platform? And the hand print on the car door? All puzzling. Of course there's also the little problem of Cleopatra."

"Darling, have you forgotten? Dogs walk. By themselves and frequently away. Now you're being silly."

"Again, possibly. But affectionate pets don't often wander away by themselves for long."

"Let's forget about it for a while, shall we?" Nora shook her head distastefully.

"Right."

Marc turned off the main highway onto a white gravel road designated by a weather-beaten sign as the road to Duck Lake. They wandered through a tunnel of trees for several miles, to come out on a slight rise overlooking the blue beauty of sunlit water shivering in a gentle breeze. The glistening sails of several boats dipped and curtsied to each other with prim politeness. A raucous speed boat threshed the water with belligerent impudence. They admired the beauty of the scene as Marc drove slowly along the road skirting the shore.

Nora sighed with envy. "Wouldn't it be wonderful to live here?"

"Nice enough in the summer, but chilly, come the cold north wind."

"Summer'd do," said Nora.

Marc studied the road. "We should be almost there. I've only been here once before, but I think we come to Richards' cottage first. . . . Yup, here we are." He headed the car into a curved driveway.

They stopped before a low stone house which, by contrast with a huge oak tree at each corner, appeared deceptively small. An expanse of lawn swept to the edge of the lake.

"People call these cottages!" exclaimed Nora with undisguised envy. "I shouldn't have come, Marc. I'll never be satisfied with the simple things again."

Marc climbed out of the car and ran around to hold the door for her. "May I remind you once more that the owner of this cottage is known as 'the late Mr. Richards'? Are you coming?"

"Try to lose me!" Nora swung her legs out of the car. "What do we do now?"

"Dangle the line to see what bites." Marc pressed the doorbell button. When considerable time elapsed without any response forthcoming, he pressed again and held it. The door was opened suddenly by Mrs. Donovan. Her thin lips were pressed in a tight line of disapproval.

"Well, young man," she snapped, "where's your manners? Can't you give a body time to get to the door?"

"I beg your pardon, ma'am," replied Marc, bowing politely, hat in hand. "I was afraid there was no one home. I wanted to make sure before we left. You are Mrs. Donovan?"

"Huh! That's better. Yes, I'm Mrs. Donovan. What do you want?"

"I'm a friend of Mrs. Joan Arnold's. She told me I'd find you here. Have you heard about Mr. Richards' accident?"

Mrs. Donovan grunted in disgust. "Yes, I've heard, but I don't believe a word of it. Some nonsense cooked up by them silly radio announcers to moan about. Saw Mr. Richards last night, and chipper as ever he was."

"I'm sorry, Mrs. Donovan, but it's true. Mr. Richards was murdered last night."

Mrs. Donovan paled. "I declare! Poor Miss Joan. Well, I can't say's I'm surprised. Who're you?"

"Marc Jordan. I'm chief attorney—lawyer—for the railroad. This is Miss O'Conner, my—ah—secretary. I'd like to talk to you, if I may."

"Come on in then; don't stand there moonin'." She led the way into the comfortable pine-paneled living room. "Might's well set and be comfortable. First time I ever used the parlor for my own company, but I guess Mr. Richards won't care now. Go ahead, young man; what do you want?"

"Have you been housekeeper for Mr. Richards for some time?"

"Nigh onto twenty-five years. I came on as Mrs. Richards' maid when they was married, and Mr. Richards got so's he could afford help."

"And you've been here ever since?"

"That's right."

"You said you weren't surprised that Mr. Richards had been killed. What d'you mean by that?"

"Well, Mr. Richards, he wasn't a easy one to get on with. Not that he wasn't nice to me," she added hastily. "Always polite and nice as could be. And gentle and lovin' with Miss Joan and Mrs. Richards—poor soul—while she was still livin'. But the other people, he was awful hard on them sometimes."

"What other people?"

"Mostly railroad men, I guess."

"That's funny," said Marc thoughtfully. "I've known Mr. Richards for several years, and that wasn't the impression I had of him at all. The working men all liked him."

"Mebby so, but he could be nasty to some of the big shots."

"Perhaps that's the way he got results. D'you have any particular person in mind?"

"No, can't say's I do."

"How about Mr. Linden? Has he been here much?"

"Not lately. He used to come out once in a while. I know for a fact they didn't hit it off good."

"Quarreled, eh? Recently?"

"Can't say."

"How about Mr. Richards and Mr. Arnold?"

"Right at first, they didn't get on so good either. But lately they been real friendly."

"Have they ever quarreled?"

"Don't think so. Whenever Mr. Richards got one of his mads on, Mr. Arnold, he just left."

"Practical diplomacy at its peak," muttered Marc dryly. "Did the Richards family have much social contact with the people next door, the Johnsons?"

Mrs. Donovan's shoulders twitched with contempt. "That brazen hussy! Makin' calf eyes at Mr. Richards! She's got her eye on everythin' in pants. Sayin' she liked to fish! I'll bet she never lifted a goldfish bowl! And that white bathin' suit of hers, her that can't swim a stroke, swingin' them hips and—and the rest of her around for everyone to plainly see! Her husband ought to take a paddle to that round behind of hers!"

Marc chuckled. "Apparently, Mrs. Donovan, you don't hold Mrs. Johnson in very high esteem."

"That I don't."

"Tell me, Mrs. Donovan, did Mr. Richards reciprocate the—er—calf eyes?"

"Don't know as I can say. He never told me, and I ain't one to pry around into other people's business. All I know it, Mrs. Johnson and Mr. Richards used to go fishin' at night a lot. Seems like they never caught much fish, neither."

"Has that been lately?"

"No, come to think about it, they was only out onct this summer. Seems like there ain't been much sociability back and forth lately."

"You said Mrs. Johnson's mean to her husband."

"Agnes—she's her maid—" Mrs. Donovan jerked a thin thumb toward the house next door, "tells me about some of the rows they have. Mrs. Johnson, she can really lay it on with that wicked tongue of hers. Agnes says they had a beaut a few days ago, only for a change Mr. Johnson, he was doin' the talkin'. Maybe he's gettin' some sense."

"Did she say what the quarrel was about?"

"She says Mr. Johnson hollered about two faces, and not standin' for it any more, and wringin' someone's neck. Mr. Johnson, he was mad."

Marc rose and slowly paced the length of the room. "Hm, yes. Did you notice anything unusual in the family affairs yesterday?"

"Nope. I didn't see much of 'em. They was eatin' on the train, so I didn't have no cookin' to do. Mr. Richards took 'em in his car, and everybody was just like always."

"Mrs. Johnson didn't go along. Did you see any activity next door after they left?"

"I didn't see no one, but Agnes says Mrs. Johnson drove off in her car, that sporty red job she's so proud of, and didn't get back till all hours. But I didn't see nothin'. I wasn't payin' no attention."

Marc arrested his slow pacing, his body tense with concentration, and his eyes glittering with suppressed excitement. He stared at Mrs. Donovan.

"So—Mrs. Johnson *was* out last night! Late! Interesting. I don't suppose she gave any explanation?"

"Said somethin' about a party with friends. Some friends!" The straight line of her lips expressed Mrs. Donovan's firm convictions about the friends. Marc's glance met Nora's. He resumed his march.

"It's really imperative that we pay a social call next door," he muttered. "Imperative. Can we get through that row of trees, Mrs. Donovan?"

"Sure. Follow the path. There's a open space through to their drive."

"Fine. Come on, Nora. We've taken enough of Mrs. Donovan's time." Marc walked rapidly to the door. "You've been very helpful, ma'am. Thank you."

"That's all right, young man. You see the police catch that feller."

Marc covered the width of the veranda in long strides, with Nora's heels tapping along behind him. They followed the path to the tight row of trees and found the opening that allowed passage through to the lawn on the far side.

Their feet crunched in the white gravel of a driveway that led to a two-car garage attached to the house. The garage doors stood open, disclosing one empty space, and the other filled by a long, sleek, black sedan. Marc paused as they walked toward the front steps, pulled out his notebook, and jotted down the license number. Stepping into the ivy-covered entryway, he repeated the bell-pressing operation.

The door was opened by a trim little maid with vacant blue eyes.

"Is Mrs. Johnson in?" asked Marc politely.

"Yes sir," replied the maid, the blue eyes surveying him with approval, "she's here, but she's resting. I can't disturb her."

"I see," he said. "Are you Agnes?"

"Yes sir," was the smiling reply.

"We're anxious to see Mrs. Johnson. I'm surprised she's sleeping at this time of day."

"Well sir, she was at a party almost all night. She said she was tired and was not to be disturbed."

"Where was Mrs. Johnson last night?"

"I don't know, sir. She just said a party."

"When did she leave?"

"About eight-thirty. She drove."

"And got back when?"

"I don't know exactly. It was getting light when I heard her. When I took up her breakfast, she said not to bother her again."

"Was she asleep then?"

"I don't think so, sir."

"Do you like it here, Agnes?"

The girl's forehead puckered in a frown. "Confidentially, sir, I'm leaving the end of the week."

"Don't they pay you enough?"

"They pay more'n I'd get most places, but there's things a girl don't have to take."

"For instance?"

"Nothing pleases Mrs. Johnson. She's forever bawling me out about something. She's mean to me, and to Mr. Johnson, and I don't like it."

"So the Johnsons don't get on so well?"

She shook her head. "I'll say they don't."

"How'd it happen Mrs. Johnson didn't go to Chicago?"

"I don't know, sir, except she ain't been exactly friendly next door."

"Have you had the radio on today?"

"No sir. That's one thing annoys Mrs. Johnson, 'specially when she's resting."

"Have you talked to Mrs. Donovan?"

"Not since early this morning. Mrs. Johnson wanted me to sort some clothes, and I've been busy."

"Who is it, Agnes? Who are you talking to?" a rich, throaty voice asked petulantly.

Agnes turned from the door, and both Marc and Nora watched with keen interest the figure descending the stairs. She was beautiful, with a full red mouth and straight black eyebrows. Her lustrous black hair was combed back to a shoulder length bob with professional skill. A red satin house coat, tied at the waist with a black sash, displayed a fluff of negligee at her throat, and a generous length of pajama-clad leg. Silver-buckled red slippers gracefully crossed the hall.

"A gentleman to see you, ma'am," stammered the flustered Agnes. "You said you weren't to be disturbed."

"Well, you've no business standing there talking to strangers," snapped Mrs. Johnson. "Who are you?" she demanded, turning to the couple in the door.

"Marc Jordan, Mrs. Johnson, and this is Miss O'Conner. I've some matters to discuss with you, if you please."

"I don't please. What business could you have here? I don't know you."

"That's my misfortune," said Marc quietly. "However, I do have business with you, of an important and confidential nature." He glanced meaningly at the maid.

"Oh, all right. Agnes, scram! Come in." With a haughty toss of her head, she led the way into a coldly modernistic room. Dropping carelessly into the corner of a yellow leather divan, she fumbled through a silver cigarette case. Tapping a cigarette on her thumb nail, she crossed her legs, disregarding the glare in Nora's eyes.

"What's this confidential business?" she demanded.

Marc's half closed eyes never left Mrs. Johnson as he, too, coolly lit a cigarette, and settled into a chair opposite her.

"Thanks for your warm hospitality, Mrs. Johnson," he said. "Agnes tells me that you've been resting all day. I presume, then, that you've not been listening to your radio?"

"It's none of your business what I've been doing. No, I haven't had my radio on. How can that interest you?"

"Obviously, it can't," replied Marc. "Just insatiable curiosity. It'll come as a surprise and a shock, then, to learn that your friend and neighbor, Mr. Richards, was murdered last night."

Marc watched her. The cigarette paused in mid-air, the green eyes narrowed to thin slits, and the expertly applied rouge stood out on her pale cheeks. There was no other sign of emotion.

"Murdered!" she exclaimed. "You don't say! Well, I'm not surprised." Suddenly stiffening, she demanded fiercely, "Who are you? Why are you telling me this?"

"As I said," Marc replied suavely, "Marc Jordan, chief attorney for the railroad. Since Richards was our president, we are naturally interested. I'm sure you realize that. It's my understanding that Mr. Richards left here last night in company with his family—and your husband. Natural curiosity leads me to hope there're things to learn here."

"Why come to me?" The green eyes darted over Marc's face.

"You're neighbors. People often know unexpected and interesting things about their neighbors."

"I can't tell you a thing. We were only casual acquaintances." Mrs. Johnson snubbed out her cigarette with vicious jabs, and reached for another.

"Please, let me judge that." Marc leaped to his feet with a ready match. He gave Nora a quick glance as he returned to his chair, and caught her look of mixed amusement and disapproval.

"I hear you like to fish, Mrs. Johnson."

"Fish? And if I do, is there anything wrong in that?"

"Not at all. Only I'm somewhat surprised. You don't seem the type." Marc allowed his glance to wander over the shapely expanse of leg.

"It's no problem to determine your type, Mr. Jordan!"

"Ah, yes, quite," said Marc hurriedly. "I wonder if you could help me identify this person." He pulled an envelope from an inner pocket. Carefully extracting a snapshot, he handed it to Mrs. Johnson. She examined the picture coldly and handed it back.

"Never saw him before in my life. Who is it?"

"That's what we're trying to find out," replied Marc, returning the picture to the envelope, and the envelope to his pocket. "I was hoping that you'd be able to help. After the rest left last night, you were out."

"And if I was, what of it? Any concern of yours?"

"Oh, not at all. There's my curiosity again. Out late. And you drove—would you mind telling me where?"

"I certainly would mind! None of your damn business!"

"I see," said Marc dryly. "I was sure you'd feel that way. Just one more question, Mrs. Johnson. Were you planning to return to Calumet soon?"

"That's none of your business either," she snapped, "but I was. I'm driving back tomorrow."

"That's fine," said Marc, rising slowly and settling his coat about his shoulders. "That'll be more convenient! May I suggest that you allow nothing to interfere with those plans? I'm looking forward to a resumption of our conversation."

Mrs. Johnson rose slowly, her half closed eyes watchfully on Marc. "I haven't the slightest idea what you're talking about."

"I'm sure you haven't." Marc helped Nora to her feet, and turned to the door. "Good day, Mrs. Johnson. You've been very kind!"

She watched in silence as they hurried across the lawn.

"Marc Jordan," demanded Nora breathlessly, "what are you up to? You've been talking in riddles all afternoon."

"Not riddles, Nora, just indirectly."

"And you were positively indecent—eyeing her like that! You never look at me that way!"

Marc grinned at her. "Would you want me to? Anyway, it was all strictly in the line of business. Pretty legs seem to loom large in this affair."

"Well, I don't like it," said Nora, pulling her coat about her. "And she's a—well, she's—!"

"Yes, she certainly is." Marc skillfully backed the car out of the driveway.

"Sometimes your manners annoy me, Marc. Usually you're such a gentleman. I don't like it when you're rude."

Marc glanced at her soberly. "Neither do I, Nora. Some people mistake courtesy for weakness. I don't enjoy being rude, but there are times when I realize it can be helpful."

"Maybe, but I still don't like it. Now where are we going?"

Marc looked at his watch. "It'll soon be time to satisfy the inner man. The pangs of hunger creep up on me. Let's head for town and food."

They drove in silence, enjoying the cool evening. Marc slowed as they circled the lake. The wind had died, and the sailboats had gone home for the night. Motionless boats, occupied by stolid, silent fishermen, dotted the glossy black mirror, and lengthening shadows marched across the water.

Arriving at the outskirts of the town, Marc drove through several side streets and finally nosed the car up to an express wagon parked on the railroad station platform. Climbing out, he and Nora entered the station and approached the ticket window.

"Mr. Jones?" asked Marc, looking up at the name posted over the window.

"That's right. What can I do for you, sir?"

"Marc Jordan. I'm with the company." Marc slid one of his cards through the grating. "Could I talk to you for a minute, please?"

"Oh, yes, Mr. Jordan. Of course. Step this way." He pointed to a door into the booth, which he unlocked. "What was it you wanted?"

"I suppose you've heard about Mr. Richards?"

"Yes. Terrible, isn't it? Old Dick was a fine one. I hope they catch the crook."

"So do I," agreed Marc. "Were you on duty last night?"

"Yes, sir, I was."

"I wonder if you remember any of the Pullman passengers who got on the Flyer here last night."

"Why, I only sold space to one passenger. A lady came up just before train time and bought space to Chicago."

"In that case, perhaps you remember her well enough to describe her."

"Well," he hesitated, "yes and no. I'm afraid I can't tell you much about her. She wasn't so very tall, about medium I'd say, and she was wearing dark glasses and a cloth thing over her head. I couldn't tell you what she looked like, except that she had right pretty legs!"

Marc shot an amused glance at Nora. "Pretty legs! Splendid. There was a woman on the train last night whose actions were—to say the least—peculiar. We've been trying to trace her. Is there a garage handy where cars, can be parked all night?"

Jones considered a moment. "Most garages around here close up at six. There's the Buick garage across the street, in the next block, stays open all night, and another about four blocks toward town."

"Fine. Thank you, Jones. No need to bother you any more."

"Glad to help, Mr. Jordan. If I can do anything, let me know."

Marc and Nora left the station and crossed the street to the garage. A lanky, pasty-faced youth sat on a rickety chair tilted against the wall, and worked diligently on a mouthful of gum.

"Hello, mister," said Marc. "You the night man here?"

"Uh-huh."

Marc pulled his hand from his pocket and flashed a bright object in his palm before startled eyes. The chair legs came down with a bang and the boy scrambled to his feet.

"Yes *sir!*"

"I want to know if a red sport coupé was parked here last night."

"Sure was. She's in here right now." He led the way through the dark cavern of a door to where a big red coupé nudged the wall of the garage. Marc glanced at it and, pulling out his notebook, wrote down the license number.

"When was this car brought in?" he asked.

"Around nine. Little later, maybe. A lady parked it. What's the matter? Is this pile hot?"

"No, it wasn't stolen—at least I don't think it was. Now the useless question—what did the lady look like?"

"She had on dark glasses and a light tan coat and—"

"And had pretty legs!" interrupted Marc dryly.

"Yeah. How'd you know?" asked the boy in surprise.

"Did she leave her name?"

"No sir. I gave her a ticket and she said she'd be back in a few days."

"O. K., buddy. Much obliged."

Marc led the way up the street in silence. They went into the coffee shop of a neat little hotel. As they sat waiting for dinner, Nora asked, "What was the picture you wanted Mrs. Johnson to identify?"

Silently Marc pulled out the picture and held it up for her to see. A handsome, blond young man leaned debonairly on a porch rail and stared impudently at her.

"Why," she exclaimed in surprise, "that's your brother Neal! What in the world did you show her that for?"

Marc smiled grimly, and returned the picture to his pocket. "A trick as old as the hills, Nora. I wanted to get

Mrs. Johnson's fingerprints without her knowing about it. I think we'll find them very nicely framed on that lovely picture of my good-for-nothing brother!"

10

Inspector Anderson sat hunched in his chair. A pudgy hand slowly massaged his shiny bald head as he glared, goggle-eyed and perplexed, at the pile of papers lying in a disordered heap on the desk before him. He thumbed through a sheaf of fingerprint sheets, noted in the scrawl of the cynical Murphy. There were prints of everyone: Richards, Johnson, Cliff, Joan; many unknown; even Jordan was included. He dumped the bundle into a file basket and picked up the doctor's report on Richards.

> *General health excellent. No organic disorders. Slightly enlarged heart normal in an athletic man. No trace of poison. Bruises on forehead, nose and right knee, probably caused by fall. Death instantaneous, caused by a severed spinal cord below the base of the brain.*

Anderson tossed the report after the fingerprints and drew a large envelope from a drawer. Arranging in an artistic arc before him on the desk an assortment of gruesome pictures, showing Richards in all the stark reality of the photographer's cold light, he sat back glaring at them and impatiently gnawing at a stump of a cigar. He was interrupted by the jangle of the telephone at his elbow.

"Yeah!" he barked. "Yeah—speaking. Who? Well, you don't say. Where's he now? Well, bring him up—bring him up. What're ya waiting for, the moon to change?" He banged the receiver back on its hook and slid down into the chair, his face alight with hope.

The door to the office burst open and a burly cop unceremoniously pushed a tall, flabby-looking man into the room.

"Here he is, Chief," said the policeman. "Come for his bag a little while ago. I picked him up like you said."

Anderson glowered at the man. His light tan suit was wrinkled and mussed. A narrow belt withdrew modestly behind tight rolls of flesh at his waist. He mopped a shiny, perspiring brow with a silk handkerchief.

"See here, what's the idea?" he blustered. "This is outrageous. Has a man no rights? I'll sue you!"

"Take it easy, buddy." Anderson bit off the soggy end of his cigar and spat it accurately into a cuspidor. "Better let me ask the questions. Sit down before you faint." He kicked around a chair into which the big man squatted nervously. "What's your name?"

"George Miller."

"And your business?"

"I represent the Morgan Drug Company."

"A drummer, eh? What're you doing in Calumet? This your territory?"

"I don't see that it's any of your affair, but I'm here on business."

"So. You're here on business. What stores you visited? What business calls've you made since you been in town?"

"None of your business," replied Miller defiantly.

"The heck it ain't my business!" Anderson thumped the desk with his fist. "You listen to me, chum. You're on a spot. You better start giving some straight answers. How come you bought a ticket to Chicago yesterday, and got off here?"

"Why, I changed my mind at the last minute, and decided to work here first," stammered Miller.

"Hah! It looks mighty fishy, seeing as what happened."

Miller looked at him in surprise. "What happened? I don't understand."

Anderson's jaw sagged open in amazement. "Good gosh, you don't mean to say you don't know what happened on your train? Where you been? Don't you even read the papers?"

"No, I didn't see a paper yesterday."

Anderson stared at him suspiciously. "All right, bud, I'll tell you. A man was murdered on your train just before it got to Calumet. Then you up and skip. See what I mean?"

Miller's arms dropped to his sides and he slumped deep into his chair, eyeing Anderson in consternation.

"Good Lord! Murder! And you think I did it!" he gasped.

"I think lots." Anderson wrathfully raked a match across the top of his desk. "You start talking. Make it fast and straight, or I'll have you booked on a murder charge before you can wink."

"But I didn't do it, I tell you, I didn't do it!" Miller whispered, wringing moist hands. "I didn't even know about it."

He was interrupted by the rattle of the door, and Marc Jordan entered.

"Well, well. A party. Anyone I should know?" he asked cheerfully.

"Blast you, Jordan, you've the manners of an alley cat!" snapped Anderson. "I'm telling the desk man to jug you, next time you start up those stairs."

"Hello, Jerry. I too am glad to see you this morning. Who's our friend?" He studied the pile of limp flesh opposite Anderson with interest. "It wouldn't be—?"

"Our fat-faced friend. George Miller, he says his name is. A drummer. Morgan Drug Company."

"How do you do?" Marc cordially extended his hand to Miller. "I'm delighted to meet you. You've caused us no little concern."

The interruption restored some of Miller's composure. His eyes darted from Marc to Anderson with both surprise and suspicion.

"You fellows are trying to pin something on me. I demand my right to consult a lawyer before answering any more questions."

"Really, I don't think that'll be necessary," said Marc soothingly. "You aren't accused of anything. Besides, if it's a lawyer you want, I'd be glad to advise you." He turned to Anderson. "What've you been doing, Jerry? Trying to browbeat this gentleman?"

"Gentleman?" exploded Anderson. "Browbeat him? How else do you treat a murderer?"

"Jerry, you're losing your grip," replied Marc. "You don't have anything on this man, and you know it." He turned to Miller. "You must excuse the inspector, Mr. Miller. He gets impetuous at times."

Anderson's face turned livid. "Jordan, I'll—!"

"Now, Jerry." Marc held up a cautioning hand. "Don't lose your temper. What were you about to say, Mr. Miller?"

"This being accused of a murder he knows nothing about, right out of a clear sky, gives a man a start. I'd like to know what this is all about." Miller's backbone stiffened visibly.

"All in due time, Mr. Miller," replied Marc.

"Say," interrupted Anderson, "where you been the last two days? You're not registered at any hotel, or did you use a phony name?"

Miller squirmed in his seat. "No, I didn't stay at a hotel. I stop here frequently and keep a room on Elm Street. It's more convenient."

"I'll bet it's convenient," muttered Anderson dryly.

" You must admit, Mr. Miller," Marc continued, "that your actions do appear puzzling. How'd it happen that you left the train at Calumet instead of going on to Chicago?"

"I've told the policeman," replied Miller stubbornly, "I had some business to attend to here, and decided at the last minute to take care of it this trip."

"Personal business, Mr. Miller?" asked Marc casually.

Miller hesitated. "Why—er—yes, I guess you'd call it personal."

"Just what could come up after you'd boarded the train? Because obviously, had it come up before you started, you'd have turned your ticket in for one reading to Calumet."

Miller squirmed and mopped his brow. "I don't see that it's any concern of yours."

"The heck it ain't." Anderson's stumpy finger disappeared into Miller's chest. "You explain your monkey shines, or, b'gosh, I'll lock you up on suspicion of murder!"

Marc blew a cloud of smoke at a fly walking across the ceiling. Miller continued his squirming and brow-mopping for several minutes. Finally he turned to Anderson.

"Can I rely on your discretion if I tell you the whole story?"

"You better tell the story and take a chance on the discretion," said Anderson dryly. "Come on, talk."

"Well, you see, my wife is jealous, very jealous. Unfortunately, she learned some time ago that I've a friend in Calumet. A very good friend—in fact, a lady friend. Whenever I go on a trip my wife comes to the station to see that I don't buy a ticket to Calumet. The only way I can fix it is to buy a through ticket and get off here. So you see, I know nothing about this other terrible affair. And you must keep my name out of it. Now, if that answers your question, I'll be going."

"Nuts!" moaned Anderson. "A fat-faced Lothario! I might've known it."

"Blessed be he who toyeth with fire, for verily, he shall be burned!" murmured Marc. "This 'lady friend' of yours, who is she?"

"It isn't necessary to drag her into this, is it?" asked Miller. "That'd be a mess. What difference does it make to you?"

"Let us decide if it makes a difference, will you?" growled Anderson. "You tell us her name."

"Well, I won't!" Miller's soft chin jutted forward defiantly. "And you can't make me. I won't say another word without a lawyer."

Anderson banged the desk with the flat of his palm. "Brother, you're going to need a lawyer—and bad! Because I'm—"

"Jerry!" Marc interrupted sharply. "Nix!" Turning his head, he favored Anderson with a slow wink. "Don't let your enthusiasm run away with you, Jerry. Mr. Miller's been very frank with us. He's obviously the victim of an unfortunate combination of circumstances, and you can get into trouble making a false arrest. His reluctance to disclose the lady is understandable."

"I can arrest him on suspicion!" barked Anderson. "And he sure as the devil is suspicious!"

"But to no end," replied Marc. "You'll just create ill will. Mr. Miller will help us if he can, won't you Mr. Miller?"

Miller looked gratefully at Marc and nodded. "I certainly will, but you see, I know nothing that'll help you."

Anderson waved his hands in a gesture of defeat. "O. K., Joe. Take him out. Leave your name and address at the desk, and don't try a run-out powder. Stay in sight. We may want you again."

As the policeman and Miller departed, Marc carefully brushed ashes from his coat and shook his head at Anderson.

"Jerry, will you never learn? Let the fly tangle his own feet in the molasses. It takes much less effort than swinging the fly swatter."

Stepping quickly to the door, he hurried down the stairs. He paused out of sight at the bottom until Miller had completed the formalities at the desk and started for the door. Sprinting to the desk, Marc made a hurried note of the address written on the blotter.

Miller turned up the street to the right, and Marc, following him, threaded his way rapidly through traffic to the other side. Miller strolled aimlessly for several blocks. Suddenly he turned into a large ten cent store. Marc dashed recklessly across the street and reached the door in time to see him heading for a row of telephone booths. Noting that one next to Miller's was empty, Marc slipped into it as a coin clanged into a slot.

Concentrating intently, he listened to the faint metallic click of the dial. Soon the faint murmur of conversation came to his ears, but strain as he would, no words were distinguishable.

After several minutes, Miller clicked the receiver back on the hook and left the store. Marc watched furtively from under his hat brim until the man disappeared. Then he dropped a coin and dialed a number. A clear voice came promptly to him over the wire. "Johnsons' residence."

Marc gasped softly. "May I speak to Mrs. Johnson— *again?*" he asked.

"Just a minute, sir."

After a brief pause an impatient voice answered, "Yes, George, what is it?"

"Dorene," mumbled Marc into the palm of his hand, "did I tell you to keep your mouth shut?"

"Of course, you stupid fool!" snapped Mrs. Johnson. "Do you think I'm crazy?"

"Sure, sure. And I'll see you—?"

"You idiot! I'll pick you up tonight as I told you. Now get a grip on yourself. They haven't a thing on us. Don't call me again. You'll get us both in trouble. Good-bye!"

Slowly hanging up the receiver, Marc stared wonderingly at the transmitter. Then, dropping another coin, he dialed again.

"Let me speak to Inspector Anderson, please," he said in reply to the query from the other end. The receiver blasted in his ear.

"Yeah?"

"Hello, Jerry. Jordan speaking. I've changed my mind, Jerry. I think it'd be a good idea to put a tail on Miller. He might know something after all. He just left Woolworth's on Main Street heading south."

"Why, you darn fool! Do you think I was weaned yesterday? I've got a tail on him right now."

"Hm. Yes of course. I just wanted to make sure. Don't lose him, will you?"

"You bet I won't lose him. That bird'll bear a lot of watching."

"O. K., Jerry. I'll see you later."

Marc walked slowly out of the store to the corner, where he stood, hands deep in his pockets, and admired the remarkable lack of shine on his shoes.

Deciding the condition of the shoes was hopeless, he headed briskly up Main Street to North and turned left. He examined the street and buildings carefully. Those buildings facing on Main Street showed, largely, blank brick walls to the side street. The other end of the block was a repetition, with the buildings facing the other way. Walking the length of the block, he came to a large automobile accessory store on the corner. Across the street on each corner was a garage. Entering the gaping door of one of them, he approached an attendant greasing a car.

"Morning, Doc," he said cheerfully.

"Howdy, mister. What's on your mind?"

Marc thumbed through his notebook. "I'm trying to trace a car. Did you ever have that number in here?" He held the book so that the man could see the number.

"Don't remember it. What kind of a car?"

"A big black Buick sedan," replied Marc.

"Nope," said the man. "Ain't had a big Buick in here for a good while."

"Do you work here every day?"

"Yup, every day."

"Then you'd be sure to know if this car had ever showed up?"

"Yup, that's right. It ain't been here."

"O. K. Thanks."

Going across the street to the next garage, Marc repeated the questioning with the same result. One by one he worked through all the garages in the neighborhood without success. Several blocks down the street he came to "Mac's Garage—Storage and Service." Mac was busy in a little cubicle of an office, laboriously writing in a ledger with a stump of a pencil. Marc showed him the number in his book.

"Good morning, Mac. D'you remember having a car with that number in here recently?"

Mac studied the number solemnly.

"Yeah, seems like I remember that one. Let's see—it oughta be in here." He thumbed through a grubby file and pulled out a card. He compared the number with the one in Marc's book.

"That's it—Buick sedan. Belongs to Mr. Johnson, president of the bank. We do all his work and store the car sometimes. What about it?"

Marc closed his book and returned it to his pocket. "Oh, I'm curious about the car. Is it here now?"

"Nope. Mrs. Johnson come and got it night before last."

"She did. Well, well. Do you remember what time she got it?"

"Around midnight. I was all set to close up when she comes in and says she needs the car."

"Are you sure it was Mrs. Johnson?"

"Oh, it was her all right."

"I wonder," Marc continued, leaning on the corner of the desk, "was that a usual thing? Did she use the car much?"

Mac shook his head. "Can't say's it was. I don't remember when she's come fer the Buick before. She has her own car—a sporty red job— she drives all the time."

"Didn't it seem strange that she should come for it at that time of night?"

"Did seem kinda funny. But who'm I to argue? Long's folks pay their bills, their business is their business, far's I'm concerned. And Johnson's good pay."

"I see. Well, thanks, Mac."

Marc hurried from the garage and hailed a passing cab. Giving the driver Miller's address, he leaned back and lit a cigarette.

The cab threaded its way into a part of town that had seen much better days. A mongrel dog ducked from under the wheels. Dirty, blank windows stared at the tin can and paper litter in the streets. The driver pulled up before a house that had once been painted brown. A wooden stoop listed at one corner, and a paper sign pinned to a grimy curtain advertised to a waiting world that the establishment was prepared to furnish room and board by the day, week or month.

Marc instructed the driver to wait and, cautiously mounting the steps, pressed the rusty door bell. After a short wait, the door was opened a crack by a slatternly, stringy-haired woman.

"Good morning, ma'am," said Marc, tipping his hat politely. "I'm looking for a Mr. George Miller. Is this his address?"

"Well, he ain't here now."

"Has he been in recently?"

"He was here last night, and night before."

"Would you tell me, Mrs.—ah—"

"Flaherty."

"Mrs. Flaherty, is Mr. Miller here much of the time?"

"What business is it o' yours?" she snapped. "I don't give out information about my guests."

Marc slipped his hand into his pocket and glanced at the bright object in his palm. Mrs. Flaherty stiffened. Her sharp eyes darted from Marc's hand to his face.

"Cop!" she gasped. "Now listen, mister, I run a respectable place. I ain't had no trouble, and I don't want none now."

"No trouble, Mrs. Flaherty," said Marc, smiling at her. "I only want a little information about Mr. Miller. Now then, is he here much?"

"He stops in fer a night every two-three weeks."

"Does he have any company? Any guests or callers?"

"Nope, never brings nobody in. I won't stand for no monkey business."

"No one comes to see him?"

"Nope. Only time I ever seen him with someone is when some dame picks him up in a big red car."

"Could you describe the lady?"

"Never seen her very good. She always wears a veil. That's some car she drives, though."

"Does he reserve the room in advance?"

"He rents by the month. He ain't here so much, so I gives him a good rate. He just drops in."

"Thank you, Mrs. Flaherty. I think that gives me the information I want. It'd be wise for us to keep our conversation to ourselves for now. Do you agree?"

"I'll keep my trap shut, if you say so," she muttered un-civilly. "I don't want no trouble. What's Miller up to that you're checkin' on him?"

"I don't know that he's been up to anything," replied Marc. "We have to check a few things once in a while. Good day, Mrs. Flaherty."

Marc climbed into the cab and gave the address of the railroad building.

11

Seated at his desk in a corner of the big office, Marc propped his feet on the window sill, leaned an elbow on his desk and gnawed on a pencil. The scene framed by the window always fascinated him. The high office building overlooked other surrounding buildings, and from where he sat, he could see one end of the passenger station, with classification yards beyond, where a yard engine puffed importantly. A coal hoist, water tank, and other less glamorous but vital pieces of railroad were spread out to the left. A lead track ran off to the roundhouse where several engines stood patiently, having their backs rubbed and their fires cleaned. The main line tracks skirted the river and curved across a bridge to disappear behind a hill. Red, yellow, and green lights twinkled along

the right of way, and the signal tower, Johnny O'Conner's seat of honor, was just visible beyond the yards.

Marc's thoughts were interrupted by a polite cough behind him. He turned to find Conductor Holland standing beside his desk.

"Oh, hello, Holland," said Marc, swinging around. "Glad you could come over. Sit down."

"That's all right, Mr. Jordan," replied Holland, dropping into a chair across from Marc. "I got your message last night when I came in on 61, but I figured that was pretty late to come over. So I got here early on the chance you might be in. I expect you're pretty busy."

Marc smiled wryly. "Busy, Holland, is a rank understatement."

"I been thinking a lot about Mr. Richards' murder, Mr. Jordan. Fact is, I ain't been able to think about much else. I guess you know how that is. Found out who done it?"

Marc scowled and shook his head. "No, we haven't. As you probably know, that's what I want to see you about. Some very peculiar things must have gone on, on that train, if you can call them peculiar. You were all shocked and upset at the time and maybe we didn't get all the facts." Marc thumbed through his notebook. "One thing that makes it tough is the fact that with a trainload of people moving around, the possibilities are almost endless. You checked the coaches. On the word of a group of sailors in the last coach, you say no coach passengers came back into the Pullman section. Do you think that can be relied on?"

Holland picked his cap off of his head and scratched thoughtfully. "I think so, Mr. Jordan. There was a bunch of them sailors, ten or a dozen anyway. They kinda took over the end of the car. You know how they do, making a lot of noise and blocking the aisle. They all said nobody went by. Anybody that did would've had to fight through them."

"How about one of the sailors slipping away without being noticed?"

"I thought of that and asked 'em. They swore up and down they'd been together all the time. It don't stand to reason that a bunch'd all gang up on a murder. The Shore Police checked 'em in Chicago, so they was on the level. I think you can bet no one from the front end come back."

"That would seem to eliminate all the coach passengers," said Marc. "It narrows the field. How about the crew? Were they all accounted for at the time of the murder?"

"Yeah. Me and Adams and the Pullman conductor and the front end brake was all setting together when Cliff come, and had been for upwards of a half-hour."

Marc referred to his notes. "That'd put you fellows together before the crime was committed. Now about the Pullman passengers."

"Blake could maybe tell you more about them than I can," replied Holland.

"But you do get back into the Pullman section, don't you?"

"Yes. Seems like I seen a fat man and a lady in dark glasses sitting together earlier in the evening."

"Is that so?" exclaimed Marc. "How'd you happen to notice them?"

"I don't know, exactly. I kinda figured they was old friends. There's pick-ups on every trip. Some guy is always shining up to a good-looking woman. Then they both start acting coy and putting on airs. You can spot 'em a mile off. These two didn't act that way. Just sat talking low, like they knew each other. I'm guessing maybe, but from Blake's description, they could be them two Pullman passengers that got off at Calumet."

"We're all guessing," said Marc dryly, "but that's a good one. We have those two spotted." He leaned back and hooked his toes around the legs of his desk. "You know, Holland, Mr. Richards was killed with a hand axe stolen from the tool case in his own car. You'll recall that we found a knife in the fountain wastebasket just inside the door from where Mr. Richards was killed. Any idea how that knife got there?"

Holland shook his head. "No, sir, I don't. I don't think none of the crew put it there."

"It's a very peculiar fact," continued Marc, "that Murphy found a woman's fingerprints on this knife. It's even more peculiar that the same prints were found on the glass of the door to that car. Strange."

Marc pivoted around in his chair and stared moodily over the busy yard. After several minutes of silence he turned back to Holland.

"Can you think of anything else, no matter how far-fetched it might seem, that was out of the ordinary? Think hard."

Again Holland shook his head.

"Is there any chance that someone slipped onto the train somewhere without you knowing about it?"

"Possible," admitted Holland, "but not likely. Us fellows always got a eye skinned for bums and such. I don't think anyone got on without us knowing about it."

"I'm afraid you're right. It looks like an 'inside job.'"

"One of the men on Mr. Richards' car got off once, but got right back on."

"He did? Where was that?"

"That'd be at Hastings. He got off and went into the station. When he came back he was unrolling a pack of cigarettes."

"Who was it?"

"I think it was the light-haired, good-looking fellow."

"Think of anything else?"

"I'm sorry, but I'm afraid I can't."

"When I talked to Miss Joan yesterday, she told me that her pet poodle, Cleopatra, became lost, strayed or stolen in the excitement at the station. Have you seen or heard of her around the yards?"

"No, I haven't, Mr. Jordan."

"If you do, let Miss Joan know, will you? She's very fond of that little dog. Thanks for coming over. If you or any of the crew run into anything, let me know."

"Sure will. Glad to help any way I can."

Marc resumed his unseeing scrutiny of the panorama spread out below, and Holland threaded his way through the office. As he disappeared, Marc reached for the telephone and dialed a number.

"Hello!"

Marc winced away from the receiver. The blast was the foghorn voice of Thatcher's guard.

"Marc Jordan. If Thatcher's there, I'd like to speak to him."

"Hold it," was the reply, followed by a short pause.

"Thatcher speaking. What's on your mind, Jordan?"

"One question, Thatcher. Yes or no, was George Miller one of the men in the life of Mrs. Dorene Johnson?"

The telephone was silent for a moment. "Yes, he was," replied Thatcher finally.

"Why didn't you tell me that yesterday?" demanded Marc.

"You didn't ask me."

"No," said Marc dryly, "I didn't. How did Miller figure?"

"Oh, he just figured," replied Thatcher. "He spent a lot of time and money on her, at one stage of her career."

"Did Richards know about Miller?"

"Of course. We reported everything to him."

"I see. All right, Thatcher. Thanks."

The smoke of several cigarettes formed a hazy cloud around his desk before Marc again picked up the telephone.

"Hello, Maisie, this is Marc Jordan. . . . Oh, you did? . . . But you flatter my voice! . . . Sorry, Maisie, I can't tell you a thing. . . . No, I don't not yet. Please place a call to Abercrombie and Coyle in Chicago. I'll speak to either Mr. Abercrombie or to Mr. Coyle. . . . Yes, that's right. Mr. Barber's out, so put the call in his office. . . . Thanks, Maisie."

Walking over to the desk where Nora was busily pounding typewriter, he tugged a loose curl straying back of her ear.

"Stop it, Marc. I'm busy," she said crossly.

"You shouldn't work so hard, Nora. It'll give you gray hair, not that it wouldn't become you. How about having dinner with me tonight, and maybe taking in a movie? There's a good murder mystery on at the Strand."

Nora looked at him suspiciously. "Is this another of your expense account invitations, one of those business and pleasure dates?"

Marc shook his head. "No indeed. This is pleasure. I want to forget tribulations for a while and start over. May I pick you up after work?"

"All right, Marc."

The telephone in Mr. Barber's office jangled insistently. Marc walked quickly into the office, closed the door, and seated himself at the desk.

"Your call to Chicago—we're ready, Mr. Jordan."

"Thank you. Hello?" replied Marc.

"Hello—hello—who's this?"

"Marc Jordan. Abercrombie and Coyle?"

"Yes, Abercrombie speaking. Who'd you say you are?"

"Marc Jordan—chief attorney, C. M. Railroad. I'm with Mr. Barber. I believe you know him."

"Oh, yes—Barber. Good friend of mine. How's the old buzzard?"

"In fine health when I talked to him yesterday."

"You fellows have to kill your officials to get rid of 'em? Aren't you civilized?"

"Looks bad, doesn't it? We've been investigating that affair, Mr. Abercrombie, and I'm hoping you may be able to help us. You've been handling the accounts for the C.M. for many years. Is that right?"

"That's right, young man. Been handling that account for a long time. Can't remember how long, offhand."

"In going through Mr. Richards' private file, I found correspondence relative to a discrepancy in the accounts some five years ago. I'm very curious about that error. I wonder if you recall it?"

"Yes, I remember. Our auditor found a shortage of several thousand dollars. We thought the books had been tampered with. About that time we got a personal letter from Mr. Richards saying that Linden had discovered a mistake, and that the shortage was being made up by Richards. Very peculiar, but that took care of it, so we dropped it."

"No further investigation or explanation was made?"

"No. I asked Richards about it later, but he brushed me off. Said Linden was stupid."

"As far as your audit went, Mr. Richards' check effected a balance?"

"That's correct."

"Do you remember the amount of the shortage?"

"Offhand, no. Be glad to look it up for you."

"If you please, Mr. Abercrombie. I'd like to know the date and amount of Mr. Richards' check. Also any other pertinent data. Now here's another matter. Included in the same file is a copy of a report by Mr. Arnold to you, discussing a similar discrepancy which exists now. You have that report?"

"Yes. In fact, Arnold was on his way here to discuss it. He's been unavoidably detained, I gather," he added dryly.

"Mere formality. What's your opinion of Arnold?"

"Smart man. Few dark spots in his past, but he came up the hard way. I'm one to give a man the benefit of the doubt, and he's done good work for us."

"I see. Will you look up that information and wire me here at the office?"

"Be glad to, Jordan. Anything else?"

"I believe not. Thank you, Mr. Abercrombie."

"Good-bye."

Marc climbed the steps leading to Anderson's office three at a time. Finding Anderson alone, he dropped into his usual chair. Anderson glowered at him for several minutes.

"Jordan," he said plaintively, "why d'you have to keep busting in here and messing up my work? I'm inspector, did you forget?"

"That's all right, Jerry," replied Marc, drawing lines in the air with his cigarette. "Glad to help any time. You're referring in particular to the case of Mr. George Miller?"

"Yes, I'm referring to Miller," snapped Anderson testily. "I shouldn't listen to you. We could've sweated some dope outa him right now."

"You could sweat him, no doubt about it," replied Marc, "but to what end? Possibly reduce his weight, but Mr. Miller's avoirdupois doesn't have much bearing on this case. No, it seemed that if Miller were given slack, and time to play it, he might show his hand. In fact, that's exactly what he did."

Anderson's eyes narrowed to slits, and he frowned at Marc. "What're you driving at?"

"I followed our Mr. Miller, and a very interesting trip it was."

"You wouldn't be here if you weren't going to tell me," growled Anderson. "Spill it."

"Ever study telegraphy, Jerry?"

"What the devil's that got to do with it?" Anderson exploded his cigar butt into the gaping cuspidor. "No, I never studied telegraphy."

"You should take it up. Interesting and beneficial pastime. Miller wandered around town a while. Then he ducked into the dime store, and headed into one of the phone booths. I remembered that I had a call to make, too, and as luck would have it, I found myself in the booth next to Miller. Did you ever pay attention to the sound of a telephone dial, Jerry? If you have a telegrapher's ear you can tell the number from the sound of the dial clicks. See what I mean? It's a good trick. Just as a matter of interest, I made a note of the number Miller called."

"By the Lord Harry," exclaimed Anderson, staring at Marc with reluctant admiration, "you got the makings of a detective! Give me that number and I'll have it traced right away."

Marc puffed absent-mindedly. "That's not necessary, Jerry. I know whose number it is. Now I'll tell you the rest of this yarn on one condition—that you make no rash moves. Promise?"

Anderson gestured helplessly. "I swear, Jordan, it's gotten to where I don't know who's running this case, you or me. What're you trying to do, steal the show?"

"Not at all, Jerry. But you aren't dealing with the usual sort of criminal, and your methods won't work. You have to use a certain finesse in this case. But you're the boss."

"Okay. I'll use whatever 'finesse' you want. Go ahead."

"I called the same number as soon as Miller left. And who do you suppose I got? Mrs. Dorene Johnson!"

"My gosh, no!" gasped Anderson. "So Miller is in on this. I thought so all the time."

"Furthermore, Miller and Mrs. Johnson have a rendezvous scheduled for sometime this evening. May lead to nothing. The mere fact that they are in cahoots is really all we need to know. However, I suggest you keep your hawk eye glued to Mr. Miller!"

"You bet I will!" Anderson barked into the telephone. "Joe! You got a tail on Miller? That guy that was just here? . . . All right, get this. If you lose him you're both fired! Got it? . . . All right, see that you don't." Anderson slammed the receiver back and turned to Marc. "What do you make of it?"

Marc shook his head slowly. "I really don't know, Jerry. Holland, the train conductor, says he saw Miller and our lady friend of the dark glasses talking on the train. Naturally he didn't think anything about it at the time. It would certainly appear that he's involved, but how, I don't know."

Anderson leaped to his feet and paced angrily around his desk. "This case is about to drive me nuts! Beats anything I ever saw. Here we've a barrel full of suspects, and not a thing to tie up any of them."

"Oh, by the way"—Marc reached into his pocket and gingerly extracted a photograph, holding it by the edges —"what d'you make of this?"

Anderson stopped his pacing long enough to examine the picture, and glanced at Marc in surprise. "Now who'n thunderation's that?"

"My brother," replied Marc lightly, returning the picture to the envelope. "Nice-looking fellow, isn't he? And a good likeness."

"What's your brother got to do with it? Is he involved too?"

"No, not exactly," replied Marc, tossing the envelope on Anderson's desk. "But his picture is—perhaps. As a favor, Jerry, and just to keep the record straight, I wonder if you'd have Mr. Murphy do his dusting act on that picture. Might be some prints."

Anderson glared at Marc suspiciously. Picking up the picture, he silently left the office.

Fifteen minutes passed. Marc sat with his hands behind his head, staring at the ceiling. His meditations were interrupted when Anderson stamped back into the room and waved the envelope under his nose.

"What goes on, Jordan?" he demanded. "This picture's got two sets of prints—yours and a woman's. Furthermore, the woman's check with those on the knife and on the window pane. Who is she?"

"Childish things, fingerprints. Crude," murmured Marc. "But none the less sometimes useful. Remember your promise, Jerry? Nothing rash!"

Anderson nodded.

"A little bird whispered our lady's name, and it'd appear the bird has excellent connections. I paid her a visit yesterday and persuaded her—unconsciously of course—to oblige with her prints on that picture. You see, your rule-of-thumb methods are sometimes worth trying."

"Yeah, but who is she?"

"In due time, Jerry. All in due time." Marc eyed Anderson through lowered lids while he exhaled several long plumes of smoke. "If I tell you now, you'll dash out and give her the business. That might gum up the works."

"Look, Jordan, I can find this dame." Anderson slumped into his chair wearily. "But you can save us time. What's her name?"

Marc stamped his cigarette against the end of Anderson's desk. "I'll tell you what, Jerry. I'll make a bargain with you. Promise to leave the lady strictly alone for—say forty-eight hours—and I'll name her. How about it?"

"How do I know you aren't pulling a fast one? What're you up to? Maybe I oughta work out on you!"

Marc shook his head impatiently. "Jerry, don't be stupid!"

"Oh, nuts!" grunted Anderson, scrubbing the top of his head in complete disgust. "Okay. A hold order on the dame for forty-eight hours. Now give!"

Marc rose to his feet and paced slowly around the room, hands deep in his pockets. Finally, stopping opposite the desk, he stared unseeingly at Anderson for a long moment.

"Now take a deep breath, and get a grip on your chair arms. Our lady of many finger smudges is none other than George Miller's girl friend—Mrs. Dorene Johnson!"

Anderson was a study in arrested amazement, with glassy pop eyes, and a slack jaw. Suddenly a heavy fist crashed on the desk and the intake end of a violent oath whistled through his teeth.

"Now take it easy, Jerry," cautioned Marc. "The only reason I told you this is so you can keep an eye on her."

"But, man, this skirt was there! If she didn't do it herself maybe she saw who did! Let's get her on the pan and see what fries out. This could bust the case wide open."

"I don't believe it," said Marc, dropping into his chair. "What do we know about her? She was there, as you say. So what? If she killed Richards we can't prove it—yet. And if she didn't but saw who did, she'll admit it when she chooses, not before. That gal's a ball of ice. It'll take more than the warmth and charm of the police department to thaw her out. There's more to it, Jerry. The lovely Dorene did quite a lot of flitting about that night. Would you be interested in the history of her expedition?"

"Don't torment me, Jordan, please!"

Marc lit another cigarette and blew a lungful toward the ceiling. "I have it from an unimpeachable source that after the others left Duck Lake for the train, Mrs. J. retired to her room, presumably for a change of attire. Then, boarding her fancy coupé, she drove to Hastings, where she stored the car. Carefully disguised in dark glasses and kerchief, she bought a ticket on the Chicago Flyer, and quietly slipped on.

"Sometime during the evening she visited the car platform—either before, during, or after the murder. Note that we've no way yet of knowing when. However, we can deduce that it was during, or after, because as soon as the train stopped at Calumet she did a vanishing act. Something must've happened on the train to change her plans—suddenly!

"She took a cab to North Avenue, walked west three blocks to Mac's garage, picked up her husband's sedan and drove back to Duck Lake. Her maid thinks she was at a party. She drove here today and returned her husband's car to the garage. To complete the picture, she'll shortly slip back to Hastings and get her own car. I'll bet that's what she'll do. It'll be interesting to find out. That's one reason I've been so insistent that you leave her alone. Let's see what she does for a couple of days."

Anderson's jaw rode morosely on his chest and cigar smoke curled around his head.

"But, good grief, man. What's she up to, sneaking around the train? No good, I'll bet a bent car check. I've got enough to hold her as a material witness, and maybe break her."

"Not that little lady. This thing's clever, Jerry, very clever. It was either a murder of impulse, and the murderer was lucky, or it was planned to the last decimal place. I incline to the latter view. Let's play dumb. Let the birds hop around a while. Maybe one of them'll show the color of his wings."

Anderson sighed wearily. "Okay, Jordan. Guess you're right. I'll have to admit you're turning up some neat points," he added. "We'll sit tight and—"

He was interrupted by an insistent buzz from the telephone.

"Yeah? . . . Who? . . . Oh, he does. Well, send him up." Banging the receiver down, he turned to Marc. "Some bird says his conscience's bothering him. Knows something that may tie in with Richards' murder. Wonder what's eating him? . . . Come in!" he bellowed, in response to a timid tap at the door.

A meek little man, clutching a felt hat tightly to his breast, his smooth round face wearing a self-conscious smirk, slipped mincingly through the door. Pale eyes darted from Marc to Anderson.

"Come in—come in," said Anderson briskly. "The sergeant says you've got something to tell me."

"Well, I—ahem—don't know that it's—ah— important, and it might be—ah—of a confidential nature. I was thinking—ah—that a conversation in private—ah—might be—"

"Oh, don't mind Jordan," said Anderson, waving his cigar in Marc's direction. "He's my pal. Who're you? What's on your mind?"

"Tomas is my name, sir. Josephus A. Tomas. I'm in— ah—lingerie and ladies' furnishings. I— ah—don't know that what I—ah—have to say is—ah—important. It has been weighing on my— ah—conscience the last two days and I—ah—"

"Hey!" snapped Anderson impatiently, "we won't bite. If you know something, out with it. Let me say if it's important or not."

"Yes, sir." Tomas dusted the underside of his chin with a lavender handkerchief. "Well, you see, I was at my summer place on Duck Lake a few weeks ago and—ah—one evening Mrs. Tomas and I decided to—ah—dine out. We went to the Kewpie Inn, a resort restaurant about thirty miles away on another lake. I just—ah—happened to notice that—ah—Mr. Richards was also dining out, in company with a very—ah—beautiful lady. It came as quite a surprise to me."

Anderson grunted with disappointment. "What's so funny about Richards taking a lady to dinner? It's done every day."

"That's true." Tomas' eyebrows arched self-righteously. "But the lady is married, you see."

"Did you recognize her, Mr. Tomas?" asked Marc.

"Oh, yes, I did. It was Mrs. Johnson. Mrs. Arthur Johnson."

Marc and Anderson exchanged a long, meaningful glance.

"Did you know Richards well?" asked Anderson. "You sure he's the one you saw?"

"I know him only slightly. We belonged to the same golf club. There's no—ah—question about it. It was Mr. Richards."

"How about Mrs. Johnson? Are you sure about her, too?"

"Oh, unquestionably. I've—ah—served her many times in my shop. She's a very striking woman. Very striking."

"How'd you happen to come here to tell me about this?"

"Well—ah—I was startled to see them together. And—ah—then when Mr. Richards was murdered I—ah—got to thinking about it. Sometimes these things lead—shall we say—to tragedy? It just occurred to me that it might help you."

"Tell me, Mr. Tomas," said Marc, watching the death throes of a fly entangled in a cobweb on the ceiling, "did Mrs. Johnson and Mr. Richards act like surreptitious love birds?"

Tomas turned to Marc in surprise. "Oh, not at all! In fact, Mrs. Johnson looked very unhappy indeed. And Mr. Richards seemed—ah—furious. I saw Mr. Richards take some papers from his coat pocket and—ah—give them to Mrs. Johnson. Later he waved them under her nose as though he were threatening her. Mrs. Johnson got up and left without eating her dinner, and—ah—Mr. Richards finished alone."

"Looked like a lovers' quarrel, eh?"

Tomas examined a tiny spot on the brim of his hat. "At least I—ah—would say it was a quarrel."

"Have you ever seen them together before, or since?"

"No, sir, unfortunately I haven't."

"It is unfortunate," said Anderson dryly. "Well, thank you, Mr. Tomas. I don't know that it helps us, but I appreciate your coming over."

"That's all right, Mr. Anderson. I'm one who—ah—wishes to see justice triumph."

"Yeah! Leave your name at the desk. I'll call you if we need you again."

Tomas slipped silently out of the door and Anderson turned to Marc, who was still intensely interested in the tribulations of the fly. Finally the fly gave up, to hang limply in a shroud of cobweb, and the patient spider darted out for his meal.

"A break, Jerry," murmured Marc softly. "A plain, ordinary, dumb luck break!"

"Mebbe so," growled Anderson. "Looks like one more nail in Mrs. Johnson's coffin. Those mash notes must've been hers after all. Say! I wonder if Johnson knew about this? He was all alone in the lounge at the time of the murder, and what a motive! By gosh, I've a good notion—"

"Hold it, Jerry," said Marc, pacing the office with suppressed excitement. "Don't do anything rash. The fog shows signs of lifting. A few of the pieces are starting to line up. But I still do not understand how— By the way, here's something I forgot."

He carefully extracted his wadded handkerchief from his pocket, and placed a ball of paper on Anderson's desk.

"I picked this out of Johnson's wastebasket the night of the murder."

Anderson glared at Marc. "I'll bet you forgot! Suppressing evidence, are you? I could hold you as an accessory, Jordan. What's the idea?"

"My apologies, Jerry, but this looked like a plant at the time. Still might be, but I'm not sure. See that dirt on the paper?"

He pointed to the loose particles lying inside the crumpled paper.

"Cast your experienced eye on that and tell me what it is."

Anderson went to a cupboard and returned with a microscope. Setting it up on the window ledge, he focused on the debris in the paper. After a brief examination he turned to Marc.

"Phenomenal! It's cigarette ash!"

"Of course. Do you have any of those letters from Richards' file handy?"

Anderson reached into one of the cavernous desk drawers and slapped a manila folder in front of Marc.

Smoothing out the crumpled note, Marc selected one of the letters and laid the note beside it.

"You see, Jerry. Mrs. Johnson was on the platform, as proved by the fingerprints. If these two samples of handwriting only matched, we'd really have a case. But they don't. They're very different. Therefore, it looks as though someone else's involved; someone we know nothing about. It doesn't make sense any way you look at it."

Anderson stared at the two letters and nodded glumly. "Yeah, I see what you mean."

Again the telephone interrupted insistently.

"Yeah!" said Anderson. "Who? Oh, Jordan. For you," he said, handing the receiver to Marc.

"Jordan speaking."

"Hello, Marc. This is Nora. I thought I might catch you at police headquarters. A telegram just came for you a few minutes ago."

"A telegram. Hm. Open it, Nora, and then use your judgment about reading it to me over the telephone."

He waited while Nora complied.

"It's harmless, I think. I'll read it to you. *Chicago, September tenth, Marc Jordan, Re telephone conversation exact shortage was 2475 dollars stop current shortage 1500 dollars stop monkey business in the coal shed indicated. Signed Abercrombie.* What does it mean, Marc?"

"I can't tell you, Nora. Thanks for calling. I'll see you later. Good-bye."

Marc hung up with a worried expression and wandered to the window, where he stood gazing out at the drab inner court.

"Jerry," he said, turning to face a puzzled Anderson, "just to keep the record straight, let's now take up the case of Mr. Eric Linden."

"Linden!" exclaimed Anderson. "I'd about forgotten him. What about it?"

"Don't believe we can afford to forget anyone," replied Marc dryly. "Let's consider Linden. I did some snooping around his past. He's a queer fish. Lonely. Almost a hermit, self-centered, a collector of old manuscripts. You remember that receipted bill of sale in Richards' private file? I paid a visit to Lord's Bookstore, and made a few judicious inquiries. That manuscript was sold, by Richards, under peculiar circumstances. He brought the manuscript to Lord to sell, and stipulated a price of $2475.00, no more, no less. Lord says that he told Richards it was worth much more. The strange part is that the manuscript had originally been purchased by Lord for Linden! Then how did it happen that Richards was selling it?

"Abercrombie, of Abercrombie and Coyle, auditors for the railroad company, just wired me that a shortage in the company books at the time of that sale also amounted to $2475.00, said shortage being subsequently made up on a personal check from Richards. Funny business.

"In other words, all signs point to the fact that our Mr. Linden, overcome by his yearning for old paper, had dipped into the company exchequer to the tune of $2475.00, and that Richards caught him at it. Richards, knowing Linden, realized that the crudest punishment he could mete out would be to force Linden to make good by parting with one of his most prized possessions. Hence the sale."

Marc paused while Anderson blinked, his brain absorbing the implications of this information.

"And moreover," continued Marc, "Abercrombie now reports another shortage amounting to no less than $1500.00, circumstances similar."

Anderson dug his knuckles into his eyes and glared at Marc in despair.

"Good grief, man, you telling me Linden's a thief, once for sure and mebbe twice?"

Marc grinned at him. "Check. And considering Linden's character, a little on the loose screw side, with years of suppressed fear and hatred boiling in him, he could easily work himself up to a state where he could commit murder!"

"That old maid secretary, Miss Arthur. She looks like a loose screw too."

Marc nodded. "Miss Arthur's an example of the sad plight of the neglected office wife! She's been burning a candle for Richards for years. Office gossip. And she's touchy about it."

"That's a fine motive."

"But why Richards?" said Marc. "Miss Arthur undoubtedly knew Richards was playing games with Mrs. Johnson. Why not kill her? Oh, I know, love turns to hate. Could be."

"Looks like everyone had reason to kill him. Now you tell me who did."

Marc resumed his pacing around the office.

"Our list's shaping up, Jerry. For instance, Linden. On his own admission, he and Richards turned in at the same time. Therefore, he's unaccounted for at ten fifty-eight when the axe hit the track at Zola.

"Item: Linden had motive and opportunity.

"Now take Johnson. He was alone in the lounge car, with Arnold on the observation platform, and unable to swear that Johnson didn't leave. Also Johnson probably knew about his wife's philanderings.

"Item: Johnson had motive and opportunity.

"Now Arnold. Richards was about to change his will putting all his money in trust for Joan.

"Item: Arnold might be considered to have motive, and opportunity, if we can figure out how he skinned the length of the car in nothing flat without being seen.

"Consider Dorene Johnson. She had plenty of motive—a very lurid past which Richards knew about. Moreover, she was boiling with the ire of a woman spurned. The only construction we can put on her tête-à-tête dinner date is that Richards was telling her off in an attempt to protect his daughter. Furthermore, she was on the train and at the scene about the time of the murder. Circumstances strange, to say the least.

"Item: Mrs. J. had motive and opportunity a-plenty.

"And Mr. George Miller, erstwhile boy friend of the lovely Dorene. He may also have had a motive. Just being an associate of Mrs. Johnson's would indicate the possibility. He also was on the train, was seen with Mrs. Johnson, and left under suspicious circumstances.

"Item: Mr. Miller had opportunity, and maybe motive.

"Miss Arthur. In love with Richards. Unrequited. The papers are full of murders committed for less. There's no check on her movements after nine-thirty.

"Item: Miss Arthur had opportunity and maybe motive.

"That leaves out Cliff and Joan. Justified, I think. Note a peculiar circumstance, Jerry. If we assume that opportunity consists in being on the car, and deduce the responses of the human brain to certain stimuli, every one of our suspects—again omitting Cliff and Joan—had both opportunity and motive. So we can't eliminate anyone. There you have it. You figure the answer."

Anderson slowly shook his head. "Jordan, Richards wasn't murdered! So help me, he died of old age!"

Marc chuckled. "You have something. But don't be downhearted. A ray of sunshine appears. In the meantime, I want to borrow the bloodstained towel found under Johnson's bunk, and the murder axe."

Anderson stared at him in amazement. "Are you crazy? I can't let you have 'em. They're evidence."

"Please, Jerry. I've a hunch. I promise I won't destroy one bit of the evidence, and I'll have them back tomorrow."

Anderson considered for several minutes. "Okay. But, brother, you have 'em back here tomorrow. If anything happens, I'll have your hide." He picked up the receiver and barked into the telephone, "Bring me Exhibits 'A' and 'B' in the Richards case."

"Thanks. If what I suspect is true—"

"What you up to, Jordan? More monkey business?"

"I don't know. It's too outlandish."

Marc gingerly wrapped the axe and towel, brought in by a languid clerk, into a neat bundle, using Anderson's newspaper.

"Hey, what's the idea, stealing my paper?"

"Never mind, Jerry," retorted Marc with a grin. "Nothing in the paper that'll help you solve this case! I can't wander through the streets with a bloody towel and axe dangling loose. One of your bright cops might jail me as a murderer!"

"If you don't get those exhibits back here tomorrow, in good shape, you'll be jugged! And how!"

"I'll take the chance." Marc tipped his hat over one eye, and strode briskly out of the building.

He entered a tall office building several blocks up the street, and rode the elevator to the top floor. Entering a door opposite the elevator, he approached a neat, starched young woman in charge of a telephone and file cabinet.

"Is Dr. Lindstrom in?" he asked.

"I'm sorry, but the doctor's out. I expect him in about half an hour. Will you have a seat, please?"

Marc glanced at the room full of patients in various attitudes of dejected resignation.

"No, thank you. I don't need the doctor's ministrations today, and I haven't time to wait. May I have a piece of paper, please? I'll write him a note."

He wrote rapidly, sealed the note, and handed it with the package to the nurse.

"Will you lock up this package, please, and see that Dr. Lindstrom gets it with the note as soon as he comes in? It's very important."

The girl smiled at Marc. "I'll give it to him as soon as I can. Who shall I say called?"

"Marc Jordan. Eric will understand what I want."

Leaving the building, Marc headed for the railroad office.

12

The motorcar clattered along the rails, pitching fretfully from side to side like an impatient steer shaking off a fly. The signal maintainer leaned over, intently watching the embankment and ditch on his side of the tracks, and Marc Jordan, soft cap pulled over his ears and coat bundled up to his chin against the chill in the fall breeze, did likewise on the other side.

"How far from Zola, Morrison?" asked Marc, shouting to be heard over the raucous put-put and clanking wheels of the motorcar.

"About twelve miles, Mr. Jordan," replied Morrison. He consulted a slip of paper. "We gotta go in the hole at Breen for Number 5."

"Any more trains after that?"

"Nope, that's all till noon. That'll give us a good shot at it. What're we looking for, anyway?"

Marc pulled his coat tighter around him and shook his head. "I'm not sure. Anyway, we're getting a lot of fresh air."

Morrison tamped tobacco into a blackened corncob pipe with his forefinger. Lighting a match, he cupped a hairy paw around the flame and expertly lit the pipe with a skill bespeaking long experience with the wind. Exhaling a trail of smoke, he grinned at Marc.

"You should be ridin' this iron when it's zero! That's when the air's plenty fresh."

Marc shuddered. "No, thanks! This is enough for my thin blood."

Morrison slowed to a stop as they approached a passing track switch. Clambering off, they lifted the motorcar onto the passing track and rolled slowly toward a group of section men who were methodically tamping ties. Marc approached the section foreman supervising the work.

"Hello, Joe," he called cheerfully. "How's track business?"

"Howdy, Mr. Jordan. Good shape. Ain't seen much o' you lately."

"That's right. I've been busy in town."

"Say, Mr. Jordan, what happened to old Dick? Fella at the roundhouse tells me he was all cut up in little pieces and throwed off the train. I ain't seen nothin' like that on my section. Musta been stringin' me, huh?"

"That's some exaggeration," replied Marc wryly, "but not a lot. He wasn't a very pretty sight. Have you been all over your section since Tuesday?"

"Let's see." Joe scratched his head and lubricated the end of a tie with a splash of tobacco juice. "Yep, believe I have. Why?"

"Find anything along the tracks that looked out of place?"

"Like what?"

Marc scowled in thought. "I don't know. It might be a small axe, or a knife—probably a large knife. There should be a towel or rag."

He glanced around at the group of men who were leaning on picks and shovels and listening with apathetic interest. One by one they all shook their heads.

"How about a black bitch poodle? She strayed away from Mr. Richards' car Tuesday night. See anything of her?"

"Well," said Joe slowly, "not a live one, but I seen a dead dog in the ditch yesterday."

Marc reached for his briar and tamped it full.

"Where?" he asked softly, turning to Joe.

"Beyond the head block 'bout a mile."

"That'd be about fifteen or sixteen miles west of Zola?"

"Yeah."

"Will you show me the place?"

"Yeah, sure."

"Hot rail!" shouted one of the men, pointing down the track. The gang stepped to safety while the train screamed by with its ears pinned back.

"Come on, Morrie, let's go," said Marc, starting for the motorcar with long, quick strides. "Hop on, Joe. Show me where you saw that dog."

The three men clambered onto the car and jerked off behind the train. After a short ride, Joe touched Morrison's arm and pointed to a spot at the foot of the bank. As the car jolted to a stop Marc jumped off and scrambled down the bank to where a small, furry black body lay partly covered with leaves. Carefully brushing away the leaves and dirt, he studied the mutilated dog from all angles. Gingerly sliding the collar around, he rubbed the dirt and tarnish from a license tag.

Marc straightened and thrust his hands deep into his pockets.

"Item: One black poodle—very dead!" he breathed, eyes glistening with excitement.

Joe and Morrison gaped at him in puzzled wonder. He walked around the dog and sighted over it, up and down the track, his face wreathed in a happy grin. Then he grasped the carcass by the tail and heaved it onto the track. Unfastening the collar, he slipped it into his pocket.

"This what you're looking for, Mr. Jordan?" asked Morrison curiously.

Marc turned the dog over with his foot. "Yes, one of the things. But then," he murmured softly, "it had to be here! Absolutely had to be here somewhere."

Morrison shook his head dubiously. "I expect you know what you're doing. But darned if I see why you run around the railroad looking for a dead dog!"

Marc squinted and looked at him quizzically. "Ah, but there you have it. Was she dead, or wasn't she? And where?" He sucked thoughtfully on his pipe and stared at the dog. "As simple as that! Only how in the devil—!"

Shrugging his shoulders, he turned to the section foreman.

"Joe, will you bury this so that I can tell Miss Joan that her pet has had the benefit of proper Christian rites?"

"Sure, Mr. Jordan."

"Thanks. Nice work spotting the carcass. Come on, Morrie; let's run to Zola. We've work to do."

Marc and Morrison squatted on the motorcar and set off down the track, leaving the section foreman to dispose of the earthly remains of the late Cleopatra.

Arriving at Zola tower after a jerky ride, they set the car off the tracks, and Marc inspected the layout. The tower was located at a crossing between the C. M. Railroad and the S. D. The tracks intersected at a long angle, with the building set in the long side of the angle. A mass of pipes spiderwebbed out at ground level and connected with the tracks. Marc walked over to the crossing and looked at the tilted parallelogram formed by the crossed rails.

"Tell me about this layout, Morrie."

"It's a mechanical plant, Mr. Jordan, run by this operator. The switches got electric locks run by the Calumet dispatcher. There's automatic indicating circuits tell the dispatcher whenever a train passes."

"What happened to you here?"

Morrison joined Marc beside the crossing.

"Well, I'm out at Perkins—that's about five miles"—he jerked a thumb over his shoulder—"on a case of trouble. We just come by there. Johnny told me to stay on account of he didn't wanta delay Number 61. So I stayed until 61 goes by, and followed him.

"I'm going through here slow, mebbe ten mile an hour. Right here I was derailed like you know about. The axe musta been laying in that lefthand corner, because I went off to the right. See, there's marks on the ties. It threw me in the clear down the bank. Skinned my hand on the cinders. I called Johnny soon's I found the axe."

Marc nodded. "I know. I was in the tower when you called."

"Oh, yeah, sure," said Morrison. "Anyhow, it looked funny. I probably wouldn't 've thought much about it, only that train had just went by. I figured it musta come off the train."

"Any possibility that it might have come from a train on the S. D. tracks?" asked Marc.

Morrison shook his head vigorously. "Not a chance. No trains on the S. D. anywhere near that time. Jake says there wasn't, and he oughta know."

"How long after the train passed before you got here?"

"Oh, mebbe five-ten minutes, I set on soon's he passed Perkins."

Marc locked his arms under his coat behind his back and rocked from heel to toe.

"When you were at Perkins, were you where you could watch the train as it passed?"

"Yeah," replied Morrison, pulling a tattered paper packet from his pocket and gnawing off a piece of plug tobacco. "Soon's 61 showed, I got in the clear and watched him go."

"Did you notice the last car?"

Morrison massaged the stubble on his jaw reflectively. "Well, I did kinda look that car over. Johnny told me old Dick'd be riding on the tail, so I was watching for him. Couldn't see much, though. That hoghead was really wheeling it!"

"Could you see anything that was going on? Think hard, Morrie. It's very important. There was a murder in progress while you were standing beside the tracks. Perhaps you were a witness to it! Did you see anyone on the car?"

Morrison's brow was creased with the furrows of intense concentration. "The back half was lit up bright like a Christmas tree. The only guy I could swear to seeing was a fellow in the glassed-in part, reading. There was light coming under the blinds of one, or mebbe two of the windows forward. Couldn't be sure about that." He thought a moment and then continued, "I think there was someone on the back platform."

"Man or woman?"

"A man, I think, but I wouldn't wanta swear to it. That platform was pretty dark. Just as the rear end passed, he straightened up, and I saw his shadow against the light."

"What do you mean, straightened up?"

"Well, you know. Mebbe he was getting up from a chair, or mebbe he leaned over to spit, or tie his shoe. I dunno. Anyhow, the shadow came up like he'd been bent over."

Marc nodded. "How about the other end of the car? That's where the murder was committed. Anyone out there?"

The furrows on Morrison's brow deepened. "It's awful hard to say, Mr. Jordan. If there was anyone on that platform, I didn't see him. I was looking at the train, but like I say, he was running like a bat outa hell and I can't say for sure."

Marc puffed thoughtfully for several minutes, while Morrison watched him.

"What do you make of it, Mr. Jordan?"

Marc shrugged. "It's queer, Morrie. The train was reported at this point at ten-fifty-eight. We can assume that the murderer didn't stand around and admire the tooling on the axe after he—or she—swung so expertly. Therefore, the presence of the axe at this precise spot seems definitely to fix the time. Then in a matter of minutes, you bust along and find it. Does that make a difference, or doesn't it? I'm darned if I know. It's very peculiar!"

Marc paused, and then added irrelevantly, "How'd you say the dog died?"

Morrison stared at him in surprise. "Huh? Why, run over. Hit by the train, anyway. She's all cut up, and her head's about off."

"Hm, yes. Looks that way. Well, let's head for Calumet."

With his hat cocked at an angle and his hands thrust deep in his pockets, Marc picked his way through the maze of tracks of the freight yard. The control tower made an oasis of light in the gloomy pall of smoke. Arriving at the steps, he slowly climbed to the tower room.

He twisted the broken-down chair around with his foot, dropped into it wearily and propped his feet against the skirt of the stove. He returned a gesture of welcome from O'Conner, who was busy manipulating a telegraph key.

Finishing the business of the moment, O'Conner spun about and favored Marc with a grin.

"Howdy, Shylock!"

Marc grunted. "Shylock, eh! Have you mixed your characters, or are you being nasty? Howdy yourself."

"You been doin' a mess of traipsin' around this man's railroad, Marc. You birds really clipped in here from Zola, this evenin'. What's the idea? You figurin' on takin' up the signal business?"

"I didn't go for the pleasure of the ride, I assure you," said Marc fervently. "They ought to spring-mount and air-condition those darn cars. What a way to travel!"

O'Conner nodded. "Yup. Them fellers can have the whole ball o' wax. Me, I'll take a nice, warm, sittin' down inside job."

He was interrupted by the clang of the gong and a winking red light on the control board. The telephone buzzed. He flipped a button on the machine and reached for the telephone switch.

"Z. A.!"

"Delton. How's Number 61 tonight, John?"

"Fifteen minutes late. Cleaned his fire at Hastings."

"Wanta do anything about Number 12?"

"Nope. Let her ride. Baxter's hoggin' it on 61. He's liable to make up fifteen minutes."

"Okay, John. Clear Number 12 with three orders, Number 8, 26, and 27."

"Clear Number 12 with three—Numbers 8, 26, and 27. Okay at seven twenty-two. J.C.O."

"Marc, you better get Mr. Richards' murder cleared up pretty quick," continued O'Conner, turning away from the machine. "Nora says you ain't fit company for a self-respectin' squirrel. You'll be losin' a nice gal friend, if she is my daughter."

Marc slid his hat over his eyes and laced his fingers around the back of his head.

"No one wants it figured out more that I do. Tell me about this gadget of yours, Johnny. How does it work?"

O'Conner settled himself comfortably in his chair and glanced at the array of apparatus before him.

"You wanta know how the guts inside work?"

"No. Just how it moves trains," replied Marc. "And how you know what goes on."

"That's good. There's a lot of stuff inside I don't savvy. You'd have to get a signal man for that. Fact is, I don't think they know either. Just stand around and look wise."

Marc chuckled. "I notice you yell for Morrison when you have trouble."

"Well, he gets overtime," muttered O'Conner defensively. "This jigger controls the main line between here and Hastings."

He pointed to an etching along the top of the board.

"This here's a picture of the track all the way. We got lights that light up whenever a train goes by, in each section of track. See, there's Delton." He pointed to a light on the track model. "Number 12 is there now." Then he pointed out of the window toward a headlight flickering in the gloom. "There's the local leavin' town, and here he shows on the board."

"Can't you move switches from here?"

"Yup. Switches and signals. Gotta lever for all of 'em."

"I thought you had a written record of train movements."

O'Conner indicated a sheet of paper mounted under glass in the top of the desk.

"Sure, on a chart. This paper's ruled off in minutes, and it's driven by a clock. There's a pen in the back for every important spot on the railroad. Whenever a train passes one of them places, it wiggles the pen and marks the chart. That shows the time he went by. Automatic. Simple, eh?"

Marc grimaced and, pushing himself to his feet, walked over to the machine. He studied the chart for several minutes.

"Now you're coming to the point," he murmured. "Any trains wandering around scratch those pens so you never lose track of them."

"That's right."

"Then it isn't a matter of someone remembering; there it is on paper."

"Right."

"How about the chart for Tuesday last? D' you have that one?"

"Yeah. They're all filed so's we can check back."

O'Conner unhooked a large folder from a rack in the corner and spread it out on the table. Leafing through, he opened it to the chart for Tuesday. He penciled a ring around a jog in one of the lines.

"There's Number 61. He went by Zola at exactly ten-fifty-eight."

Marc pondered the chart silently.

"No argument about it, is there?" he said finally. "That's what I thought."

He stretched out again in his chair and glared at the stove.

"Johnny, you've worked around here a long time."

"About forty years," replied O'Conner.

"You probably know everyone who's worked on the railroad."

"I know a lot of 'em. Why?"

"Did Eric Linden ever work in the signal department?"

O'Conner considered. "You mean that pussyfaced feller that's treasurer or something?"

"That's the one."

"Don't know as he ever worked for the signal department, but he worked different places. Started as a telegraph operator, I think, and was clerk in the traffic department a while."

"Has he ever been up here?"

"Oh, sure." O'Conner spat accurately at the open ash door of the stove. "All the big shots been here. Old Dick was right proud of this job and he was forever droppin' in.

All the brass hats on the railroad was here a coupla months ago."

"Was Johnson in the party?"

"President of the bank? Yeah, he was along."

"I see." Marc stood up and stretched lazily. He walked to the door, and waved to O'Conner. "So long, Johnny. Much obliged."

Starting across the tracks, Marc barely avoided being hit by the rear end of a train backing quietly toward him. He picked his way cautiously in the dark and headed toward a siding at the far edge of the yard where Mr. Richards' private car had been parked. As he reached for the rail to climb into the car, he was blinded by a stabbing beam of light shining full in his face.

"Goin' somewhere, buddy?" growled a gruff voice.

Marc blinked in the bright glare.

"Yes, I'm going into this car, Officer. Will you please take that light out of my eyes? It hurts."

"Who're you? My orders are, nobody goes into this car."

"A wise precaution," said Marc, fishing in his pocket for his wallet. "Jordan. Here's my pass card. I'm working on this case with Inspector Anderson."

The policeman focused his light on the card proffered by Marc. Then, flashing the light back to his face, he nodded.

"Oh, yeah. I remember you. You was here when we found the body."

Marc smiled. "Right. Now may I go in the car?"

The policeman scratched his jaw dubiously. "Well, Anderson said nobody, but I guess it's all right for you, since you're on the force, in a manner of speakin'."

"Thanks, Officer. I'm sure Anderson'll support your decision. Smoke?"

Leaving a slightly befuddled minion of the law to puff a cigarette, Marc mounted the steps and entered the car;

the same steps and the same car that had held such a gruesome shock for him only a few days before.

He found Cliff, chair tilted against the wall, deeply
engrossed in a comic magazine. His feet hit the floor with
a thud as Marc opened the door.

"Oh! Howdy, Mistah Jawd'n. Di'n' spect to see yo'."

"Hello, Cliff," said Marc. "I thought you'd be taking
care of things."

"Yas suh. Mis' Joan, she say stay heah."

"There's one question I want to ask you, Cliff. Did you
deliver a note to Mr. Richards Tuesday evening?"

Cliff bobbed his head. "Yas suh. I did, suh."

"Where'd you get it?"

"F'm Andrews."

"And where'd he get it?"

"He say some lady tol' him to git it to Mr. Richahds
'thout anybody seein' it. So Ah slips it to Mr. Richahds on
the sly."

"Did you see the lady?"

"No suh."

"Okay, Cliff. I want to look around again. I see you've
cleaned up."

"Yas suh. Dat p'leeceman say he wuz through his snoo-
pin' an' scratchin' 'round, so Ah's shined her up. Kin Ah
he'p yo', Mistah Jawd'n?"

"No, I'm afraid not, Cliff. I've some thinking to do."

Marc walked slowly along the passageway, examining
the details of the car. He opened the door to each room as
he passed, and looked in.

Entering the lounge, he snapped a light switch and
flooded the luxurious furnishings with soft light. The litter of the last evening of occupancy had been removed. No
speck of dust marred the bright surfaces. The brass had
been burnished and the rugs cleaned.

Marc dropped into the end of the davenport with a sigh, and stretched his legs out. He was reclining against the soft cushions in this position when Cliff softly stepped through the door.

"Mistah Jawd'n, suh, wud yo' all lik' a cup o' coffee an' a—"

Marc leaped to his feet and strode toward the startled porter. Placing his hands on Cliff's shoulders, he shook him gently.

"Cliff!" he breathed. "You son-of-a-gun! That does it."

Marc rapidly paced the length of the lounge and back, while Cliff stared at him in round-eyed wonder.

"What—what—?" he gasped.

"Cliff, you've given me the last piece to this jigsaw puzzle. How stupid of me. It's just as plain as day. Now, Cliff, here's what I want you to do."

13

Marc leaped from the car step and hurried across the yard to the station platform where his battered Ford was parked. Closing the car door, inserting the key in the ignition, stepping on clutch and starter, all in one skillfully synchronized motion, he spun the car around the station circle. He hesitated briefly at the thoroughfare entrance, then headed for the business district.

A grim smile curved his lips and thoughtful furrows creased his forehead as he guided the car through the early evening traffic. Arriving at a large office building, he carefully pulled into a convenient space between "No Parking" signs and headed for the entrance.

He found the doctor's office full of people in various stages of despair. Dull eyes were turned on him in annoyance. The nurse greeted him with a smile.

"Is Dr. Lindstrom in?" he asked.

"The doctor hasn't returned from the hospital, but I expect him at any minute. Won't you be seated? There are several ahead of you."

He grinned and shook his head. "Thank you, no. I left a package for him this morning and I'm very anxious to have his report."

"Oh yes! Of course, you're Mr. Jordan. The doctor left the package for you, and a note in case he was out when you called."

She unlocked a drawer and handed Marc the package. He tucked the envelope into his pocket, the package under his arm. Thanking her, he quickly extricated himself from the ether atmosphere.

He climbed into his car just as a policeman with a parking ticket glint in his eye bore down on him, and joined the stream of beetles in the street. He negotiated a succession of traffic jams, threaded his way across town, and pulled up beside the City Hall.

The officer on duty glanced up as Marc entered the dingy corridor.

"Go on up; he's there," he said, jerking a thumb toward the stair. "But be ready to duck! The boss's low tonight."

"Thanks," grinned Marc. "Send for the wagon if you hear any loud bumps."

He opened the door to Anderson's office and found him seated at his desk, chin on chest, his round face wearing an expression of complete frustration. Marc slid the bundle across the desk and dropped into his usual chair.

"Evening, Inspector," he said. "You look fit as a jellyfish. Your property. Item—exhibit 'A,' one bloodstained axe. Item—exhibit 'B,' one bloodstained towel. Returned in good condition and undamaged."

"Hm," growled Anderson, glaring at Marc. "What the devil are you doing, Jordan? What did you want those things for?"

"For a little experiment," replied Marc casually. "And successful, I might add. Not exactly the last straw, but a straw none the less. How's the investigation?"

Anderson heightened the shine on his bald pate with a red handkerchief, and scowled.

"If you're asking for information, it's no good. Frankly, Jordan, much as I hate to admit it, we're stuck. Damn it, I used to think I was a pretty good cop, but this case has me stopped. Not a thing to go on. Not a lead that makes sense."

Marc tamped his pipe and puffed thoughtfully.

"This is a tricky murder, Jerry. A neat combination of good fortune and forethought. And, by golly, it almost worked!" He continued smoking in silence for several minutes. "Jerry, I can name the murderer?"

Anderson jerked forward, his face a mask of blank amazement.

"Jordan, are you kidding?"

Marc slowly shook his head. "No, Jerry, I'm not kidding. I know who killed Mr. Richards. But I can't prove it."

"Well, come on, come on! Who was it?" Anderson leaped to his feet excitedly. "We'll grab him and sweat it out."

Again Marc shook his head.

"It'd never work. Not with this character. I'm convinced that there's not one shred of actual, positive evidence to convict this person. If you try third degree, all you'll get will be clever evasions. Everyone involved in that car had both opportunity and motive for murder—except Cliff and Miss Joan who had no motive. The guilty one knows that as well as we do, and would argue the point from here on in. What we must do is set a trap, and then flush our fox into it."

Anderson slumped into his chair in disgust. "Oh! I get it. You're going prima donna on me, eh?"

Marc hoisted himself to his feet and walked the length of the office.

"That wouldn't be sarcasm, would it, Mr. Anderson? I'm just as anxious as you are to catch the bird. Here's what I want to do. I want all the principals in this case at Mr. Richards' car tomorrow night at about nine o'clock. It should be after dark. I want them all—Linden, Arnold, Miss Joan, Johnson, Mrs. Johnson, Miss Arthur, and George Miller. Will you arrange for that?"

Anderson's cigar bounced from one corner of his mouth to the other. "What the devil are you gonna do—start a game of poker?"

Marc, arms locked behind his back, stopped across the desk from Anderson and grinned at him.

"In a sense, yes. I want to conduct a class in murder, and see which one of those choice characters'll prove to be the star pupil. Who can tell, maybe we'll have some fun."

Anderson threw up his hands in resignation. "Okay, Jordan. I'll try anything once. It's your show. I can guarantee they'll all be there!" he added grimly.

"And I'll practically guarantee that you'll have a good use for a pair of handcuffs. Now pull your chin off your tie. You're getting it all wrinkled."

"Why don't you hold these shenanigans in the morning? Why does it have to be at night?"

"In time for the afternoon papers, eh?" said Marc dryly. "For a very special reason which'll develop as the evening progresses—I hope. Let the scribes rave another day. They'll have fun, and you can slap them down harder. Wear that cat-has-the-rat-in-the-corner face of yours, and string 'em along. You'd better keep a sharp eye on our little friends, though. Someone could try a disappearing act."

Anderson shrugged. "Have it your own way. But I make the arrest, see?"

Marc smiled at him. "Definitely! See you tomorrow, Jerry."

Cheerfully whistling "My Wild Irish Rose," Marc ran down the stairs, saluted the officer on his way past the desk, and climbed into his car.

He headed through back streets to avoid traffic, and worked his way to a quiet section of the city, mellow with age and respectability. He slid into a vacant space in the basement garage of an old mansion that had been rebuilt into apartments. The Ford gave a last tired gasp and settled down for the night. Marc climbed to his third floor apartment, his feet keeping time to the "Rose."

The sound of running water, accompanied by much blowing and slapping of bare flesh, filled the room. He dropped his hat over the horn of a deer's head above the fireplace, and flung his coat over a chair. Then he kicked off his shoes and sank onto one of the beds with a sigh.

After several minutes of bathroom symphony a pair of laughing blue eyes, surrounded by a happy, round face and capped by crinkly black hair—at the moment undergoing a vigorous toweling—peered around the door jamb.

"The Great Sleuth! In the flat-footed flesh, so help me! Hark ye, evildoers. Permit not the lamps of Jordan to fall upon thee, else verily thy days are numbered!"

"Nuts," said Marc calmly, lighting a cigarette and flipping the match in the general direction of the fireplace.

"Hist!" A chubby finger crooked and pointed at the wash bowl in horror. "A beetle! And in the throes of death! Come find the guilty villain who did this deed."

"You're a psychologist. Psychoanalyze him. Maybe he's a discouraged misanthrope. Or maybe his gal friend done him wrong. He probably took a sip of that junk you put on your hair."

"Mister Jordan. You malign me—cut me to the quick. Dr. Anthony Bodine, practicing psychiatrist, my friend. Does your wife misunderstand you? Do you see black spots before your eyes? Do you have trouble finding a seat on the bus? Do your friends leer at you? Do you bite your fingernails? Come to Dr. Bodine. For five bucks a throw he'll gladly tell you to lay off that rotgut!"

Bodine walked into the room, his chunky body radiating glowing health. "On the side I dabble in mind reading. You have a self-satisfied smirk spread all over your homely map. Did you do it?"

"Well, Tony," said Marc mockingly, "do some more of your mind reading, and tell me about it. You admit that you're the lad who can."

Bodine snapped his fingers disdainfully. "To be sure, a mere trifle. But why tax my brain with such inconsequential

drivel which others of lesser intellect are capable of handling? Indeed, important matters demand my immediate
attention," he said, glancing at the clock and doing an
exaggerated toe dance to the bathroom, with the towel
functioning as all seven veils.

"Who is it tonight?" asked Marc, "Annabelle, or Ger-
trude?"

Bodine's face reappeared in the doorway, frothing with
lather. "Mathilde—ah, sweet Mathilde!" He wafted a kiss
from the tips of his fingers toward the ceiling. "Hair with
the sheen of golden corn silk and the sweet scent of roses!
Eyes—such eyes—and a complexion like a peach, floating
above the figure of Venus. And, man, can she dance!"

Marc snorted. "Hair freshly shined at Betty's Beauty
Shoppe. Complexion right off Woolworth's counter; scent
and eyes ditto. Where you pick up these flea-brained
women of yours, Tony, and what fun you get out of them,
is beyond me."

"My friend," jeered Bodine, "you're not really serious.
Flea-brained indeed. And what business has a woman with
brains anyway? It just develops psychoses, inhibitions,
maladjustments, etc. etc. What does your sweet, demure
little thing say when you mention the Kat Klub? 'Oh,
Tony, it's too expensive!' Rats! She's dying to go, but she
has her eye on a little cottage in the country. Deep, hidden
motives. Not Mathilde. 'Cover the noggin and let's go,'
she says. That's for me."

Marc chuckled derisively. "Rats yourself, Tony. You're
talking through your hat and you know it. Even the great
doctor will one day come to the little cottage. That's a
prophecy."

"Your eyes are off focus. Stow the morbid thoughts for
the evening and join us in some fun-some frolic. We seek
the haunts of light and laughter, and trip the light fantastic.
Call Nora and persuade her that a bout with the eggnog

would cleanse her soul. Better yet, trust yourself to the tender mercies of Mathilde and one of her unrepressed friends. You might enjoy it, and will you learn about life!"

"That's the trouble," said Marc dryly. "No, thanks. Now if all I had to do was figure out other people's troubles the way you do, that'd be different."

"Is the big investigation preying on your mind? My, my. Bad. Very bad. My office is full of guys like you. Their fingers shake and they jump when the cat meows. You should relax. That's a doctor's order—worth five dollars between the hours of nine and four. But to you it's free. I'm selfish. My friends'll be asking, 'Who's that old goat you live with?' Hard on my reputation."

"Nothing I do can hurt your reputation, just so I don't have to get you out of any jams, in the legal sense of the word, or try to deduce which of your glamorous pals stuck a knife into you."

Bodine strode jauntily into the room and posed before the long mirror, carefully adjusting a sky blue tie into the folds of a soft gray shirt. Touching a comb to his hair judiciously, he topped it with a gray fedora, which also required meticulous arrangement. Knotting a white silk scarf around his throat, he slipped into a black topcoat, and did a jig step to the door. Turning with one hand on the knob, and the fingers of the other pressed to his chest, he bowed formally.

"*Adios,* my good friend. I go now to seek the king of pleasure. It tears my heart to leave you thus, steeped in the mundane worries of a misguided world. I'll drink a toast to your ultimate salvation. Farewell!"

He stepped through the door and closed it quickly in time to stop the telephone book which banged against the panel.

14

An air of tension filled the luxurious lounge. The principals in the Richards case awaited the curtain call in various stages of annoyance and apprehension.

Arthur Johnson sprawled in a big chair against the forward partition where he had sat reading on the fatal night. With great concentration he spun a charm about on his watch chain and completely ignored his wife Dorene, seated beside him.

Dorene, pert hat perched jauntily over one eye, puffed on a cigarette. Her crossed legs displayed a generous expanse of silk. A red spot danced in each cheek, and a high-heeled pump beat a silent tattoo on the thick carpet.

George Miller sat across from her, his pudgy hands thrust into his pockets, and stared morosely at nothing.

Eric Linden squirmed beside him, crossing and uncrossing his knees, and wringing his hands as though washing off a stain. His pale eyes darted around the car from face to face.

David Arnold smoked quietly in the corner of the davenport and occasionally patted the clasped hands of Joan who, composed and pale, sat beside him.

Miss Arthur huddled, almost crouched, on a chair in one corner and dabbed a handkerchief to her lips.

Inspector Anderson stood, spraddle-legged and belligerent, against the rear door, puffing furiously at a long cigar. A shining expanse of forehead showed below a hat pushed back on his head, and short arms gripped behind his back pulled the buttons on his vest taut. He glared around the car, and impatiently consulted his watch.

Marc appeared at the aisle door and surveyed the assemblage, a suggestion of a smile twitching the corners of his mouth.

"Where the heck you been?" demanded Anderson. "You said nine o'clock and here it is twenty after."

Marc grinned at him. "I'm sorry, Jerry. A few last minute preparations delayed me. Well, I see everyone's here. Quite a distinguished gathering. It's good of you all to come."

"What d'you mean—good of 'em to come?" growled Anderson. "The police department had a hand in that, and I must say it took some persuading!"

"Yes, I presume it did," replied Marc dryly. He turned to Joan. "I know you want this matter cleared up. I hope it won't be too hard for you."

"I'll be all right, Marc," said Joan quietly. "The sooner you get it over with, the better. If I can help, I'll be glad."

"Thank you, Miss Joan," replied Marc, shedding his coat and hat and dropping them over an end-table.

Nora, with a murmured apology, slipped to the rear of the car and sank demurely into a chair.

"Take it easy, Jerry. You'll bite that stogy in two," said Marc.

"Nuts!" snapped Anderson. "I don't set no store by this monkey business anyway."

Johnson looked up from his watch charm twirling and asked coldly, "Jordan, would you mind enlightening us on the reason for this nocturnal party? Anderson says it's your idea. What do you expect to prove?"

"It's outrageous!" cried Dorene. "What are we, a bunch of crooks to be ordered around by the police?"

"Definitely outrageous," interrupted Arnold. "But if Anderson and Jordan feel they can make any progress—notably lacking to date—we shouldn't begrudge them our co-operation."

"I'd like to know why I'm included," said Miller. "I'm just an innocent bystander."

"Possibly that'll develop as we progress," said Marc. "It's understandable that you're all wondering why this consultation has been called. We're going to take up the subject of murder. In particular, the murder of Mr. Richards on this car a few evenings ago. Incidentally, we may delve into history."

Marc slowly loaded his pipe, tamping each flake of tobacco into position with his forefinger. Touching a match to the bowl, he exhaled a cloud of smoke and, wandering to the end of the car and back, took up a stand at the forward end of the car. He surveyed the battery of eyes turned toward him.

"First, let us review the events of Tuesday last, three evenings ago," he said. "Let me say at the start that this is a fact-finding gathering. If any of you disagree with anything I say, or have facts to add, please feel free to interrupt at any time." He paused a moment, sucking on his pipe, and then continued.

"Let's consider the surface ripples, the things we all know about, or will admit. Mr. Richards planned to go to Chicago to attend a meeting of railroad officials. Miss Arthur, as usual, went along and you, Mr. Johnson and Mr. Linden, were accompanying him to the meeting. Mr. Arnold was going to Chicago on business for his company, and Mrs. Arnold went along for the trip.

"Previously, all of you, with the exception of Linden who was in St. Paul, were vacationing at Duck Lake. Linden took the regular train and joined the party when the private car was picked up at the Duck Lake siding about seven-thirty. The rest of you drove to the car in Mr. Richards' station wagon.

"Soon after leaving Duck Lake, Cliff, Mr. Richards' porter, served dinner, which I trust was enjoyed by most of those present. After dinner the men decided on a game of bridge to while away the time. Everyone moved around quite a lot, wandering about on various errands. Cliff served drinks; Miss Arthur sat; Miss Joan read the paper; her little dog Cleopatra scampered about the car. All in all, a picture of wealthy people traveling in luxury.

"By the way, Miss Joan, did you know that the section men found Cleopatra? She'd been—ah—run over."

Joan nodded. "Yes, I know. Mr. O'Conner called me about it this morning."

"To continue," said Marc, "about nine-thirty, you got bored, Miss Joan, so you decided to go to bed. Bidding the men good night, you withdrew to your room, and Miss Arthur followed you.

"The bridge game continued another hour and broke up at about ten-thirty. Almost immediately, Mr. Richards and you, Linden, went to your rooms—and presumably to bed."

Linden nodded his head vigorously. "That's right. And I did go to bed at once."

"Hm, yes," murmured Marc. "Possibly you did. Anyway, we're agreed that you went to your room. Johnson, you sat in that same chair you're in now and read. Is that right? Arnold went out on the back platform for a breath of air. Coming in a little later, he smoked for a few minutes, and then he too went to bed, leaving you here alone. Let me see, I believe that time is accurately fixed." Marc consulted his note book. "Yes, eleven-seven according to your watch, Mr. Johnson. Tell me, how did you happen to have that time to such a close, odd minute?"

Johnson shrugged. "You ought to know, Jordan, that these railroad men live by the tick of their watches. Associating with them, I've gotten into the same habit."

"Then tell me something else. Are you familiar with the details of operating this railroad?"

"Not in details," replied Johnson. "In a general way I know how it's run."

"You've been in the signal tower and around on inspection trips with Richards?"

"That's right, I have."

"I see," continued Marc. "Now the train passed Zola Crossing at ten-fifty-eight. That's definitely fixed by an automatic chart in Johnny O'Conner's signal machine. A few minutes later Morrison, signal maintainer out on a case of trouble, had his motorcar derailed at Zola Crossing by a small, bloodstained axe, later proved to have been taken from the tool case on this car; proof that the murder must have been committed just previous to ten-fifty-eight. At that time Arnold was on the back platform, at the other end of the car from Richards, and unable to swear, Mr. Johnson, that you did not leave the lounge. And Linden was in bed, he says, as was Miss Arthur. That seems to leave you three at loose ends, at about eleven o'clock."

Linden's face turned green and he slumped down in his chair, his eyes glazed with terror. Johnson started forward, an exclamation on his lips. Marc raised a restraining hand.

"Wait a minute—no accusations yet! So far we've mentioned the surface ripples. Now let's look at some of the undercurrents."

Marc planted himself in front of Linden and frowned at him. "For instance, you, Mr. Linden."

Linden shrank away, and returned Marc's gaze helplessly.

"You were in St. Paul—on business, you say. You visited a number of banks. On the face of it not a particularly sinister pastime, we'll admit. However, it develops that you were attempting to borrow a considerable amount of money—about fifteen hundred dollars—as a personal loan. How long have you been buying rare books from Lord's Bookstore, Mr. Linden?"

Linden cringed and started as though jabbed with a pin. "Why, I—that is—"

"Never mind," continued Marc. "Merely an academic question. The length of time is immaterial. The fact is, you've spent a lot of money there—quite a lot. It might interest you to know, Linden, that a strange sequence of events has come to light. It would appear that about five years ago, the accounts of the railroad company were short twenty-five hundred dollars. The interesting fact about that shortage is the manner in which it was cleared up, namely, by a personal check from Mr. Richards. And by a peculiar coincidence, Mr. Richards obtained exactly this amount from the aforementioned Mr. Lord through sale of a manuscript—your manuscript! You follow me?"

Linden pawed his sagging jaw with nervous fingers. "Your insinuations are—ah—"

"Yes, yes, I know: slanderous. But that's ancient history. Let's skip to the present. After a brief lapse of time, your collecting urge was renewed. You recently purchased from Mr. Lord an original 'Pickwick'—for a scandalous price. Now it seems that history's repeating itself, because the last audit showed the company books again short. I wonder how that can be? Any idea, Mr. Linden? No, I'm sure you haven't, so I'll tell you. You've been embezzling money from the company treasury to satisfy your collector's mania. Years ago Richards caught you at it, and made you pay by turning over to him the manuscript, which he sold.

"But your appetite's insatiable. You tried the same stunt again, and again Richards caught you. This time there was no way out for you. Richards was prepared to prosecute, and you were really in a jam. Wouldn't it be a delightful solution—for you—to bury the hatchet in Richards' back?"

A sigh whistled from the spectators in unison. Linden's face turned livid, and he clutched the arms of the chair.

"You devil!" he snarled. "You're framing me! I'll say nothing until I see my lawyer."

With a slow shake of his head Marc stopped Anderson, who was bearing down from the far end of the car at his handcuffing gallop.

"My, my," he continued blandly. "We've progressed to lawyers in no time at all! I suggest you follow your hunch, Mr. Linden, and consult a good one—soon. You're going to need legal advice. However, we don't yet have the whole story."

Marc walked the length of the car, followed by a battery of hypnotized eyes, and stopped before Miller.

"For instance, you, Mr. Miller."

Miller returned Marc's stare coldly, drops of perspiration on his fat upper lip his only sign of emotion.

"Your presence and actions have caused us no end of speculation. It seems most irregular that a passenger would purchase a railroad ticket—particularly a Pullman ticket—and then use about one third of it. To be sure, you explained about a jealous wife, but why not make your amorous stopovers on the return trip? So much easier to explain that you were delayed a day or so, particularly since it appears that your stops are sufficiently frequent to justify maintaining a permanent address—of sorts—in Calumet. Your leaving the train at Calumet has all the earmarks of a sudden decision, precipitated by some unusual occurrence. Now I ask you, what occurrence can be more unusual than murder? What've you to say, Mr. Miller?"

The perspiration spread to Miller's forehead and his lips drew to a white line. "Nothing. You're just guessing."

"Mr. Miller," Marc chided him, "you malign me. But to continue, there was another will-o'-the-wisp riding Number 61 that night, in the form of a presumably beautiful woman. Presumably beautiful, because her eyes were marred by dark glasses, and her hair was tied up unbecomingly in a kerchief. It has been definitely established that she had very pretty legs!"

Dorene uncrossed her legs and slid her skirt over her knees. Marc ignored the interruption.

"This lady also did a vanishing act; in fact, took some pains about it—riding a cab to a side street and walking away from it. The part that'll interest you, Miller, is that you were seen in earnest conversation with the lady earlier in the evening. It might be helpful if you would identify the phantom."

"Don't be stupid," replied Miller.

"Indeed," murmured Marc. "It's a fault I struggle to overcome. Let's digress for a moment. Fingerprints sometimes enter, even as in this case. Some very intriguing fingerprints were unearthed. A beautiful hand print appeared on the glass of the rear door to the car ahead of this one. That is, the door to the platform on which Richards' body was found. Astonishing as it may seem, the same prints—a woman's left hand—appeared on the handle of a villainous knife found in a wastebasket just a few feet from the murder spot. Now why would a woman drop a knife—innocent of any marks of violence—in that basket? To establish a complicated and indirect alibi? Possibly."

"Pardon the interruption, Jordan," said Arnold coolly, "but where's all this leading? It's getting late and you don't seem to be making any progress."

Marc whirled around to face Arnold. "I'm sorry to be taking up your time, Mr. Arnold," he said sharply, "but I want to bring us all up to date. Perhaps then we *will* make progress."

He watched Dorene Johnson snuff out a red-stained cigarette butt and add it to the pile in the ash tray beside her. Snapping open a gold case, she replaced the cigarette with another. He then continued slowly.

"Let's examine the actions of our phantom lady in more detail. It appears that she purchased a ticket to Chicago, and boarded the train at Hastings. The agent happened to remember her because she was the only Pullman passenger that night. It also appears that she arrived at Hastings shortly before train time via a sporty red roadster, said roadster being parked at a nearby garage."

Marc pulled at his pipe for a moment, and then turned to Mrs. Johnson.

"I wonder, Mrs. Johnson," he said slowly, "whether it's entirely co-incidental that you drove off in your red roadster about eight-thirty Tuesday evening, and were gone most of the night?"

Dorene's face paled and the red spot burned more brightly than ever. "That's a base insinuation!" she snapped, darting a glance at her husband, who stared at her blankly. "I visited friends for a while, as I told you."

Marc nodded. "So you did. But something about that trip puzzles me greatly. Perhaps you'll be able to enlighten me. When I called on you at Duck Lake Wednesday afternoon, your maid volunteered the information that you'd driven away in your roadster at eighty-thirty, returning in the small hours of the morning. When I saw you late in the afternoon, you were still in déshabillé, having spent most of the day in bed. Now, how did it happen that your red roadster was not in the garage at that time, but your husband's sedan was parked in its place?"

Dorene gasped. "I don't know what you're talking about."

"I'll tell you," replied Marc grimly. "I'm talking about the fact that as soon as the rest of the party left Duck Lake, you went to your room, packed a bag, slipped out to your car, and drove off. You drove to Hastings, where you parked your red car in a garage across from the railroad station—where I saw it the next day, and checked the license number. You 'disguised' yourself in dark glasses and a head kerchief. You bought a berth on the Chicago Flyer, and quietly boarded it when it stopped at Hastings.

"You were recognized by George Miller, one of your pals from way back, and talked with him. You bribed Andrews to deliver a note to Cliff, who was to deliver it to Mr. Richards. You thought no one would know that you are ambidextrous as the result of an injury to your right elbow while you were part of a vaudeville knife-throwing act, so you wrote the note with your *left* hand to disguise the handwriting. You thought that would be safe, even if the note was later found.

"A few minutes after eleven you sneaked into the car ahead, and went to stateroom 'A'—which you knew from Andrews was vacant—to keep your rendezvous with Mr. Richards. You went there to murder him—with a knife! When you found he wasn't there, you went on to the platform, perhaps reasoning that that was a better place anyway. Correct, Mrs. Johnson?"

Dorene seemed to shrivel into her chair, and Arthur Johnson leaped to his feet furiously.

"Jordan," he snarled, "this is devilish slander. You haven't any proof of these accusations!"

With stiff fingers pressed against Johnson's chest, Marc firmly pushed him back to his chair.

"Please be seated, Mr. Johnson. I'll get to you in a minute. You're involved, too, don't you know. I can prove what I say. Your wife fell for one of the oldest tricks in the detective business. I asked her to identify a picture of my charming and irresponsible—but innocent—brother, which of course she failed to do. But she left lovely prints of her beautiful fingertips on the back of the card, which by strange coincidence match the prints on the knife, and the door glass."

Johnson glared at Marc malevolently. "Don't say another word, Dorene. This fool's trying to find a goat."

Marc whirled back to Dorene, who was swaying slowly from side to side.

"That platform wasn't a pretty sight, was it, Mrs. Johnson?"

"I didn't kill him—I didn't!" she moaned.

Marc watched her in disgust. "Possibly not, but given half a chance you would have. You were a little late. One of the least pleasant aspects of this case, Mrs. Johnson, has been the necessity of delving into your private life. Your career has been, at the very least, artistic! Distasteful as it is, I find it necessary to review some of the salient features of your past, for example your life in Chicago.

"You were rather more than intimate with Mr. Arnold and Mr. Miller during that period, to mention only two, were you not?"

"How'd you know that?" whispered Dorene. Johnson watched Marc through the slit eyes of a cat.

"All documented, I assure you."

"I resent your insinuation in linking my name with Mrs. Johnson," interrupted Arnold. "That was just a schoolboy infatuation. Joan knows I was no lily white angel."

Marc shook his finger under Arnold's nose. "Allow me to point out, Mr. Arnold, that Richards' knowledge of your past associations comes pretty close to providing you with a murder motive. Please don't be too hasty with your resentment."

Turning back to Dorene, he continued. "Then along came Arthur Johnson, the answer to a maiden's—that is, the answer to a prayer. You immediately assumed an air of respectability.

"Skipping to the present, you found yourself living next door to the Richards' summer home at Duck Lake. Operating true to form, you made a pass at Mr. Richards—a fascinating, handsome, dynamic man. For a short time your efforts were successful. When Richards wanted to break off relations with you, you tried to hold him. Not being a man to stand for foolishness, he had you investigated, with the result that he learned these things I've mentioned. About a month ago, he took you to dinner at a road house near Duck Lake, and flashed a private detective's report, threatening to turn it over to your husband if you made trouble."

"Damn you, Jordan," growled Johnson, "you're saying things that'll get you into trouble."

Marc spun around to Johnson. "Do you realize, Mr. Johnson, that unless you're inordinately stupid, you knew about these goings-on? Enough, at least, to have an excellent motive for murder. One of the best! And don't forget that you also had a golden opportunity. I haven't, nor have I forgotten that your wife had a similar motive and opportunity!"

Anderson interrupted impatiently. "For Pete's sake, Jordan, come to the point. All you're saying is that everyone had motive and opportunity. We knew that all the time. You aren't going to catch this bird with bedtime stories. If that's the best you can do, let's go home. I'm tired!" He angrily stamped the length of the car and leaned his shoulders against the partition.

Marc smiled at him tolerantly. "Jerry, you're so impetuous. What's your hurry? The evening's young, and I'm sure everyone's fascinated by this discussion. Isn't that so?" His glance swept the battery of tense, sullen faces.

Ostentatiously pulling his handkerchief from his pocket, he mopped his brow. Then he dropped into the vacant end of the davenport next to Joan, and started to re-load his pipe. Laying the pipe on the edge of the big ash tray, he stood up and stretched lazily.

"What time is it, Jerry?" he asked casually.

Anderson consulted his watch. "Nine-fifty-five," he replied.

Marc walked leisurely to the end of the car and disappeared down the aisle. Puzzled glances were exchanged in silence during the brief interval until he strolled back, and returned to his seat on the davenport.

"What time is it, Jerry?" he asked again.

Anderson stared at him in bewilderment, and again consulted his watch. "I just told you—nine-fifty-five!"

"Oh yes," murmured Marc. "So you did." He picked up his pipe and touched a match to it. "How long was I gone, Nora?"

Nora looked at a stop watch that had been concealed in her lap under her handbag.

"Just twenty-three seconds."

"Cliff!" called Marc.

The white-coated porter ambled into the lounge from the aisle, slowly massaging the back of his head.

"Dog gone, Mistah Jawd'n. Yoh nevah sed nuthin' 'bout sockin' me ovah de haid wit a club!"

"Sorry, Cliff. I was a little over-enthusiastic, perhaps. Tell us what happened."

"Yo' mean jist now—out on de platfohm?"

Marc nodded.

"Well, when yo' shooks yo' han'kerchief, Ah goes in Mistah Richahds' room an' waited lak yo' sed. 'N'en Ah goes to de platfohm an' jist stands dere. Purty quick yo' come out 'n socks me ovah de haid, 'n opens up de othah do', 'n goes back in. 'Ats all Ah knows."

"Look under the bunk in the room Mr. Johnson used, and in the wastebasket. Bring in anything you find."

Cliff disappeared briefly, to return dangling a brown-stained Pullman towel in one hand, and a crumpled ball of paper in the other. He handed them to Marc.

"Were these things there this afternoon, Cliff?"

"No, sah! Ah cleaned out dis evenin', 'n' dey wa'nt dere."

Marc dropped the towel and paper on the floor, clasped his hands around one knee, and flashed sharp eyes around the car.

"The murderer came from this car," he said slowly. "He sat where I'm now sitting, and saw Richards' reflection in the window when he left his room to keep his date with you, Mrs. Johnson, just as I saw Cliff a moment ago. Thus he knew precisely the second for the act.

"He followed Richards to the platform, swung the axe, threw it out the window, pitched the bloodstained towel under the berth and the note in the wastebasket, and went to his room. All in less than thirty seconds—even as I just did. That accounts for the fact that there was no apparent loss of time.

"That's about the way it was done, isn't it, Arnold?"

Instantly pandemonium broke loose. Arnold leaped to his feet with a snarl, fumbling under his arm. Anderson charged from the end of the car, and locked powerful arms across Arnold's elbows. Both of them sprawled face down on the floor. Marc kicked Arnold's wrist, sending a gun skittering under the davenport.

15

Nora O'Conner, face alight and eyes shining with excitement, perched demurely on the edge of a chair in Inspector Anderson's office. She gazed at the soles of Marc's shoes, which reared majestically above the corner of the desk. Inspector Anderson, his short legs dangling over the edge of his tilted chair, rocked back and forth happily.

"Well, we got him!" he grunted. "I always did think Arnold was the man with the axe. A mean one, he is. But I'll be jiggered if I see how you figured out it musta been him. And why all the prittle-prattle and monkey business? Why didn't we just pick him up?"

Marc blew a funnel of smoke rings toward the ceiling.

"Because we couldn't prove a thing on him, Jerry. There was literally no shred of conclusive proof or evidence against him. It was a beautifully planned job, and if Arnold had stood his ground instead of blowing his top, he could still have bluffed it through. We had to trap him, and startle him into giving himself away. All the rest was window dressing to build him up emotionally to a point where a sudden shock would catch him off guard." Marc chuckled. "It was an awfully thin chance, but it came off!"

Anderson nodded. "Yeah, but there's a lot that don't make sense to me. Where did Miller and Johnson and Linden come in? And how do you account for the fact that the axe was dropped at Zola at ten fifty-eight, when the murder was committed at eleven-seven? I don't get it."

"This murder was really planned—worked out to the split second. Let's look at the motive first.

"The relations between these people are involved to a degree. That pot has been simmering for years, and emitting a noxious aroma. One very offensive ingredient was Mrs. Dorene Johnson. It started years ago in Chicago where she met Miller, and Arnold, and finally Johnson. Heaven only knows how many more there were. She's a peculiar type who can't stand to lose any man. She's been seeing Miller regularly. Hence his sub-rosa visits to Calumet, and his hangout in that rookery on Elm Street. She's been playing

Arnold and Richards at the same time. Dangling men amounts to a mania with her. Only in Richards she met her match. When he tired of her and she started to make trouble, he promptly put Thatcher on her trail, with the result that he learned the details of her lurid past. He intended to use this knowledge as a club to shoo her off, and keep her quiet. He knew that one thing she wouldn't do was take a chance on losing any part of Johnson's bank roll.

"An unexpected by-product of this situation, as far as Richards was concerned, was the discovery that there was a link between Dorene and his daughter's husband. Old Dick was nobody's fool, and this development must have set him to thinking. He added up two and two, and decided to change his will, putting all his money in trust for Joan. That would eliminate any possibility of Arnold getting his claws on it. And there you have the real motive for the murder—the one that was used! Arnold had to kill Richards before he signed that will, or lose all chance of ever getting any of the money.

"His plan was a masterpiece. He had decided to kill Richards some days ago—probably decided as soon as he learned about the change in the will. He pondered the locale, the time and place, at some length. Duck Lake was very bad because it would narrow the field, and make it hard to establish an alibi. Calumet or Chicago had much the same limitations.

"At first glance, the train would appear hopeless, because of the cramped quarters, and the fact that he would have to account for any lost time to his wife. However, he figured out a solution to that problem. He was familiar enough with train operation to know that every few minutes a train's location is recorded automatically on a sheet in the dispatcher's office. His plan was to peg the time of the murder by dropping an especially prepared axe at some point along the line where it would surely be found, and where the train's time would be recorded. There are many such points and it could be any one of them, depending on how things developed. He probably had all such points catalogued in advance. Thus with the crime timed in advance—to the second—he could at leisure slip out any time—ten minutes or an hour later—and do the actual job. With luck, the murder wouldn't be discovered until the train arrived at Chicago in the morning. The police would time the crime by the planted axe, for which instant he would have a perfect alibi. The fact that he left his wife for a few seconds at some time after the murder was supposed to have been committed would appear inconsequential.

"He was prepared with a spare axe or a heavy knife—something small enough to be concealed in his clothes. He even had the method of fixing the phony axe all worked out. When he went out on the platform—for a smoke, he said—he held the door open for a minute, and out scampered Cleopatra, Miss Joan's little poodle. Once on the platform, he calmly killed Cleo, smeared the axe with her blood, and dropped it off the train! A little later he did likewise with the dog's carcass, making it appear that she had fallen off, and been run over.

"However, when it came time for the pay-off, he tried to take advantage of some unexpected breaks. He did some improvising in an attempt to provide a likely suspect or two, in addition to his alibi.

"When he got off the train at Hastings to buy cigarettes, whom should he spot slipping on board but Dorene Johnson, under a very thin disguise? Now, Arnold knew Dorene intimately, and understood every facet of her character. Aware of her mood and predicament, he could easily deduce that she was up to no good.

"During the course of the bridge game, further proof of his surmise materialized in concrete form. Cliff delivered a note to Mr. Richards. Richards read the note and dropped it into the ash tray. Flecks of ash were still stuck to it when I found it. At the first opportunity, Arnold retrieved the note. This told him that Richards could be expected to leave his room shortly after eleven o'clock. This was a beautiful chance, because it narrowed down the time for the crime, and made it possible to do the actual killing on the platform, thus admitting all the passengers on the train to the select list of suspects.

"As soon as Richards and Linden retired, he started his program moving. He casually strolled out on the back platform, allowing Cleo to go out too. He killed the dog and planted the axe at Zola Crossing. Then he wandered back into the lounge and sat in the end of the davenport where he could watch Richards' door in the window reflection. As soon as he saw Richards, he got up and stretched, telling Johnson that he guessed he'd go to bed. Johnson, being subconsciously time-conscious, obligingly looked at his watch and commented on the time.

"Victory number one.

"Then he slipped out to the platform and chopped Richards down, disposing of the real weapon by hurling it beyond the limits of the right of way into the woods, dropping the incriminating note into Johnson's wastebasket and the towel under the bunk, and went to his own room. He watched his wife carefully as he came in, and noted with satisfaction that she glanced at her clock.

"Victory number two, and his alibi was complete.

"The beautiful part of it was that he never once mentioned time, or seemed at all interested in it. His soul must have swelled with pride and satisfaction at his good luck, and a job well done!

"But he made one—just one—fatal blunder. The implication of that blunder, floating around in a nebulous haze from the first, didn't sink in until yesterday. How could it be possible, as indicated by the position of Richards' body and the line of blood drops—probably deliberately furnished—for the murderer to drop the axe out of a window at the front end of a speeding car in such a way that it'd pass under the car, and end up in a corner of the crossing rails, with the handle partly over one rail in position to derail a following motorcar? It can't be done. Therefore the axe that we found *must* have been dropped from the rear of the car! In his preoccupation with having the decoy axe found at Zola, Arnold made the mistake of dropping it between the rails. If he had dropped it to one side, his whole plan could easily have worked. Therefore, the person on the back platform when the train passed Zola must be guilty—namely, Arnold.

"I borrowed the axe and towel from you yesterday, Jerry, so that Dr. Lindstrom could analyze the blood. It turned out to be animal, as I knew it would. Being methodical to a degree, Arnold had the towel in his pocket, along with his real weapon, so that he could wipe up any blood that spattered about on the rear platform. The strange disappearance of Cleopatra has puzzled me from the beginning.

"One thing had me stumped, and that was how Arnold knew the precise second to go after Richards. Cliff solved that one unwittingly last evening by coming out of Richards' door while I was sitting on the end of the davenport. From that position, a reflection of Richards' door is faintly visible in the window at the side of the car. Arnold sat there until he saw Richards come out, and went after him. As simple as that. And there, Inspector Anderson, is your murder case."

Anderson sat staring at his desk top for several minutes. Then he said slowly, "Jordan, I take my hat off to you, and take back any uncomplimentary remarks made during the investigation. That's a nice piece of work, and I'll admit I'd probably muffed it."

"I don't think so, Jerry. I know a little more about railroading than you, and spotted the weak points. You'd have gotten him in the end."

Marc stretched luxuriously.

"Nora, darling," he said, "it's been quite an evening. Let's go and pick up some food."

"That would suit me," she said, smiling.

Together they ran down the stairs, and Marc waved to a respectful desk man. Clambering into the Ford, they headed across town, Nora snuggled against Marc's arm.

"How can you be so smart?" she murmured. "I'm proud of you, Mr. Jordan."

Marc grinned down at her. "I'm rather proud myself, if you want to know the truth. Holy smoke!" he exclaimed, slamming on the brakes and skidding to a stop at the curb.

"Marc, what's the matter?" gasped Nora, stiffening in surprise.

"You know that dead cow I was going to ask your father about? Forgot all about it!"

Nora sank limply into the corner of the seat, peals of laughter rolling from her lips.

About the Author

Robert Mark Laurenson (1906-1982) wrote three mysteries. He had no training in writing, but after growing so disgusted over one mystery he read, he decided to write a better one. That became his first book, *The Case of the Railroad Murder*.

Laurenson was born in Illinois, and worked as an engineer for railway companies. At the time of his second book was published, in 1949, he and his wife lived in Verona, Pennsylvania, where he worked for the Union Switch and Signal Co. From 1949 to 1970, he was the superintendent of communications at the Frisco Railway, working from Springfield, Missouri. After 1970, he retired, but continued consulting for the railway.

His first two books, published with Phoenix Press, featured railway lawyer Marc Jordan. The third, *Better Off Dead,* published with Arcadia House, was a stand-alone mystery.

The Case of the

Six Bullets

R. M. LAURENSON

**Also Available
Coachwhip Publications
CoachwhipBooks.com**

WHITE

FOR A

SHROUD

DONALD CLOUGH CAMERON

NARROW
GAUGE TO
MURDER

CAROLYN THOMAS

**Also Available
Coachwhip Publications
CoachwhipBooks.com**

**VULTURES
IN THE SKY**
A HUGH RENNERT MYSTERY

TODD DOWNING

Also Available
Coachwhip Publications
CoachwhipBooks.com

Also Available
Coachwhip Publications
CoachwhipBooks.com

MURDER IN THE
FAMILY

NICE
PEOPLE
MURDER

Mary Hastings Bradley

**Also Available
Coachwhip Publications
CoachwhipBooks.com**

A JUDGE MASSIE
MYSTERY

THE CORPSE IS
INDIGNANT

DOUGLAS STAPLETON
and HELEN A. CAREY

Also Available
Coachwhip Publications
CoachwhipBooks.com

Also Available
Coachwhip Publications
CoachwhipBooks.com

BLOOD-RED
DEATH

MINNA BARDON

Also Available
Coachwhip Publications
CoachwhipBooks.com